T0063338

FORGOTTEN KINGS

OMRI-LAND

HELEN CASS

Order this book online at www.trafford.com
or email orders@trafford.com

Most Trafford titles are also available at major online book retailers.

Printed in the United States of America.

ISBN: 978-1-4907-4688-3 (sc)
ISBN: 978-1-4907-4690-6 (hc)
ISBN: 978-1-4907-4689-0 (e)

Library of Congress Control Number: 2014916805

Scripture quotations marked NIV are taken from the Holy Bible, New
International Version®. NIV®. Copyright © 1973, 1978, 1984 by International
Bible Society. Used by permission of Zondervan. All rights reserved. [Biblica]

Trafford rev. 09/23/2014

 www.trafford.com

North America & international
toll-free: 1 888 232 4444 (USA & Canada)
fax: 812 355 4082

CONTENTS

Based on historic fact and the events of the Bible in:

1Kings 16 to 17

2Chronicles 16

Blood dribbled slowly down the blade of the dagger and splashed lazily onto the floor, time had paused...frozen in that moment, everything was forgotten except the hypnotic sadistic pleasure Zimri felt. Relishing in the sensation, he watched his masterpiece intently as the blood pool around his victims spread with a sluggish steadiness. Slowly, he looked up from the life-blood spilling onto the floor where the two bodies lay crumpled, and wiped his blade clean on the first victim's expensive purple robes. He spat on the ground deliberately next to the bodies, his spit mingling with the blood, a further insult to the dead, and he felt no remorse for his actions, just a man doing what needed to be done... a man taking out the garbage. He had come to Arza's house for this single purpose. He was not afraid to take what he wanted and he wanted the crown of Israel...

CHAPTER ONE

Tirzah, Israel.
884 B.C.

Zimri's spirits soared, he had to stop himself from jumping for joy at the fortuitous circumstances that were unravelling around him. He grinned wickedly as he thought about what had suddenly come within his grasp. The plan was coming together almost effortlessly. In fact, the whole sequence of events leading up to this moment had practically tumbled into Zimri's lap, begging to be set into motion, refusing to be ignored.

He was the commander of half of the chariot force in the army of Israel and his warriors were undeniably loyal to him. They were an elite fighting brotherhood, brave, brutal and fierce in battle, disciplined and deadly from their speeding chariots.

Earlier in the year, his entire unit had been commanded by King Elah to remain behind during the siege in Philistia. Normally such a specialized fighting force would take serious offence at having to perform the menial task that they saw as babysitting the king, a duty usually reserved for the junior un-blooded recruits and the old worn out war veterans who were unable to be of any further use on the battle field because of age or former injuries.

Initially the soldiers had grumbled at their orders, they still felt a little cheated at being left out of the siege, losing the opportunity for heroic bravery and the promise of plunder and eternal glory, but Zimri saw an ambitious opportunity to gain an advantage and he couldn't afford to let a chance like this pass him by.

He kicked out absently at a loose stone on the road, sending it skipping into the long dry grass beside the hard packed dusty path that he was casually strolling along towards the outskirts of the city. He appeared to be consumed by his thoughts while wandering aimlessly, but in fact, his mind was razor sharp and focused on the goal. He attracted no unwanted suspicion dressed in his simple tunic, with only his sword belted loosely around his hips and without his tell-tale armour to identify his rank to the local peasants.

He continued unhurriedly until he knew he was out of sight of the city walls, and then with a sudden burst of speed, he ducked into a copse of trees beside the road and ran quickly through the heavily wooded section until he came to a small stream. Launching himself over the two-meter wide gently flowing water, he rested for a short while allowing his breathing to return to normal. His first day of recognisance was going well so far and Zimri sneered, permitting himself a moment of self-satisfaction as he carefully settled himself under a large bush from where he would be able to observe his quarry.

Sweat trickled down his temple, the intense heat searing him and he reached out and grabbed a nearby pomegranate laying on the ground. Using his knife he split the ripe fruit open and enjoyed the sweet juicy refreshment immensely.

His thoughts turned to the newly appointed general of Israel's army, he knew that Omri had disliked him from the moment the two of them had first crossed paths. He knew it like he knew how to breathe, like he knew how to walk, he didn't know how he knew it, he just did. It was second nature to him, a gut instinctual ability to read the subtleties in the behaviour of those around him and Omri had an annoyingly sanctimonious attitude that grated against every single fibre of Zimri's being.

He felt that Omri always seemed to be conspiring against him, always just one step ahead and outwitting him at every opportunity. Omri had somehow gained the moronic king's confidence which had given him the upper hand in their on-going vendetta against one another.

A slave girl walked briskly out of the house he was watching, he held his breath and froze, laying absolutely still. Her robes were faded and thread-bare, she carried a large pottery jug to the well at the centre of the beautifully manicured garden. Zimri watched silently as she placed the jug carefully on a smooth well-worn rock placed beside the well as a handy table. she lowered the leather bucket down into the well, drawing water for the household while singing softly to herself and her melodious voice carried through the hot still air to where Zimri lay as she filled her jug with the cool clear water. Quickly, the girl guiltily splashed a hand full of the crystal clear liquid over her head to cool down, making the dark tendrils of escaped hair around her face curl and glisten, dripping tiny shining droplets onto her bare sun-kissed shoulders.

Zimri felt his terrible dark urge hit him suddenly. 'Not now,' he groaned softly to himself, 'I need to focus, there's no room for error, I can't be distracted…no matter how tempting that tasty little morsel appears.' With an extreme effort of will, Zimri watched the young girl walk slowly to the back of the large house before turning the corner and disappearing from his sight. He lay quietly in the cover of the bush for a long time carefully noting the movements and routines of the domestic surroundings and his mind inevitably turned back to thoughts of his nemesis, Omri.

He knew that it was Omri who was behind the royal orders to have his force stay behind and left out of the upcoming battle. King Elah had whined and used the pathetic excuse that Zimri's men should remain in Tirzah to protect the city against any attacks from another enemy in the area who might try to take advantage of Israel's main army being away in Philistia fighting at Gibbethon.

Omri's suggestion had obviously seemed very logical to the King because Israel was constantly being plagued by opportunistic enemies from the regions around them and a strong force left behind in the capital would be a deterrent to any invading army looking for a vulnerable target, but on the other hand, Zimri felt that Omri had cunningly left him behind instead of his son Ahab, who was Zimri's counterpart, the commander of the other half of the elite chariot force and was just as capable a warrior to defend the city.

Omri had also slyly chosen to omit the crucial little detail that the entire army could be back in Tirzah within a matter of two days if they rode hard and fast enough from Gibbethon, a smaller detachment could arrive back much sooner if not slowed down by the large numbers of the men in the full infantry and cumbersome baggage train.

CHAPTER TWO

Moab was a constant threat and Judah to the south was a permanent thorn in Israel's side with raids and border disputes in villages and small commercial centres on the outskirts of the kingdom taking place almost daily. Had it not been for the plan emerging in Zimri's fertile mind and the opportunity that presented itself from remaining behind, with no one looking over his shoulder during the siege, he would have been extremely annoyed and resentful at the missed chance of shedding blood in the chaos of battle.

Zimri enjoyed the camouflage in the heat of a clash; he could be openly brutal and bloody, killing for his own sadistic pleasure, giving in to his dark lust for blood in new and imaginative ways, trying to slice his opponent using painfully different techniques to torture and maim while staying just out of reach of the enemy's sword, it was always a challenge Zimri met with extreme pleasure. He often killed slowly during an encounter, loving the sound of dying men screaming and moaning around him, and it never seemed to arouse any unwanted suspicions, or so he believed. If anyone did ever notice his unusually gory behaviour, it could be easily laughed off and dismissed by him as the heat of battle in the brutality of war.

On one occasion when Israel was fighting against the Phoenicians in the Valley of Jezreel just outside of the wealthy city situated there, Zimri had separated a young Phoenician soldier from the main battle ground. He had feigned cowardice and had run from the battle field in terror just like a spineless deserter would have done, the inexperienced but brave Phoenician gave chase seeing an opportunity to kill a weak frightened enemy, an easy target, and blood his sword for the first time, gaining honour and glory for himself easily, but that had been Zimri's intention all along and he expertly sprung the trap like the predator that he was.

As soon as the two of them were out of sight of the main armies, obscured behind a line of trees, their swords clashed together, steel flashed in the brilliant sunlight and a bead of sweat ran from under the Phoenician's decorated helmet. The boy's dark hair was plastered against his forehead with sweat and his eyes began to register the fear he felt. The boy realised he was doomed and outmatched almost immediately but fought on heroically regardless. Seeing his death mirrored in Zimri's murderous eyes and knowing that it was only a stroke of good fortune that would spare his life that day.

The Phoenician was a talented swordsman. With his skills and plenty of practice, the boy might one day have almost equalled Zimri's level of expertise. He was dressed in the armour of the higher ranking Phoenician officials and Zimri guessed that he was a son of one of the generals, promoted because of lineage and birth and trained for battle since the moment he could walk.

The adrenaline surged through Zimri's veins at the thrill he felt and the scent of certain death in the air, he danced lightly around his young prey encouraging the youth to lunge towards him with sly deceptive moves, creating openings he wanted the boy to take advantage of. He had concealed his skill and pretended to be a much lesser fighter, feigning fear, which bolstered the boy's confidence and gave him some false hope as he lunged into another opening that he could not resist. Zimri swiftly stepped aside at the last possible second just brushing his razor sharp blade against the enemies exposed neck and nicking the main artery as the boy stumbled past him.

The youth didn't even register the deadly wound until he saw the blood streaming down his chest and over his sword arm and then he began to feel abruptly weaker, the blood flowed steadily making his fingers slick with the sticky red ooze, filling the air with a sharp coppery metallic scent.

Zimri killed him unhurriedly, watching intently, teasing his foe, taunting him to thrust and lunge again and again towards him and each time the young Phoenician tried to attack him, Zimri, gracefully danced just out of reach, driving the youth viciously to push the last drop of strength out of the pulsing red gash in his neck, with each movement becoming more sluggish.

The weight of the boy's beautifully jewelled sword became more then he could bear, his arm shook as he tried the lift the magnificent weapon, his armour weighing him down and each tiny effort all contributed to the enemy's heart rate rising, forcing the last of his life-blood out of the small but precise incision.

Zimri cherished the memory of that young and courageous Phoenician who had given his every fibre fighting a cause that was lost before it had even truly began; he claimed the young man's sword as his own to keep as a trophy and a constant reminder of the bloody fight, as well as the gratification and release he had felt that day.

The Phoenicians had tried to claim the Jezreel Valley for themselves but they were routed by the well-trained and disciplined army of Israel, they fled back in defeat to their strongholds in Tyre and Sidon with their tails between their legs like the cowardly dogs they were. They had tried to take the Valley by force, seeing that the Israelite king was weak and the moment to attack was optimal, a temptation to enticing for them to ignore, but their defeat would hopefully serve as a bitter reminder and deter any further attempts of conquest in Israelite territory for the near future.

The Valley was the largest in Israel and its promise of huge wealth was extremely attractive to the neighbouring nations. Its vast fertile plains lay at the foot of Mount Carmel, which is not a single mountain but a mountain range spanning for about twenty-one kilometres long in northern Israel. This range forms a massive natural defensive wall on the south side of the Valley and trade caravans and armies traveling to or from Egypt along the popular coastal route must travel through one of the several

Carmel mountain passes, which when properly managed would give an income of huge wealth from tolls and taxes along the roads to whoever holds the area.

The hills surrounding the Valley were beautifully lush with thick forests and vegetation, fields, vineyards and orchards flourishing mostly due to the moist winds blown in constantly from the Mediterranean Sea. A very prosperous piece of territory that supplies enormous amounts of produce to the nation that controls it, as well as wealth from the tolls in the passes, a constant and bottomless income in every way.

The Valley was constantly coveted by many nations looking to add to their own countries wealth and the useless King Elah had almost carelessly lost it because he was unwilling to acknowledge that the area needed more military protection. Omri had mobilized most of the army at the last possible moment while King Elah was passed out after a night of heavy drinking and debauchery, his depraved drunken orgies were legendary throughout the entire region.

Omri had risked the displeasure and wrath of the king who could have ordered his immediate execution for disobeying orders, but he had gambled his life and had secured the Jezreel Valley and surrounding area for the good of the kingdom of Israel. He was highly praised by the people and honoured by the king who had gone along with public opinion and had overlooked the slight insubordination. Instead Elah had rewarded the ambitious Omri with the promotion to the illustrious position of General of the Army.

Zimri roused himself from his pleasant reflection of the blood covered Phoenician boy and touched the sword hanging from his leather belt at his hip, stroking the jewelled hilt lovingly and smiling with satisfaction as he caressed his favourite trophy. He knew there were other strong warrior units like Ahab's charioteers that could have stayed behind to defend Israel during this siege, but Zimri refused to let it bother him any longer, thinking instead of the crown he desired and the throne he would seize.

The sun was sinking below the horizon and the cool evening breeze gently ruffled the damp dark hair on Zimri's head. He decided to head back towards the road before he lost all the fading light. 'Nothing worse than fumbling around in the pitch dark,' he admonished himself quietly, 'once I know my way around a little better, I can stay a bit longer.' Rising slowly and stretching his stiff and cramped muscles, he began to silently and stealthily make his way unseen back towards the city.

Zimri considered his strategy once more, analysing the details and searching for any weak points, but he could find none. His charioteers were now the only warriors left in the city except for the few existing old and tired soldiers on the Kings guard, who, were already more loyal to Zimri than to the alcoholic King Elah simply because they could not respect a king who couldn't rule the kingdom. There was no one there to oppose him and if need be any opponents could be quickly despatched at the flick of a sword. It was the opportunity of a life-time. Zimri smiled again, a slow, lazy calculating smile as he thought about how everything had turned in his favour at last.

CHAPTER THREE

A FEW DAYS EARLIER...

Tibni, Zimri's trusted friend was bitterly complaining one evening in their favourite brothel about the new decree that King Elah had recently enforced. The entire kingdom was to turn to the Canaanite and Egyptian deities, and they were all expected to begin worshipping the Golden Calf god that their ancestors had worshipped for generations beginning in Egypt. There was also a new Phoenician High Priest in the city preaching about a strange 'Baal' that the citizens were ordered to blindly accept and pay homage to.

The Israelites had adopted the 'bull-god' called 'Apis' from Egypt during their enslavement there. The bull was a symbol of fertility and strength and the Canaanite calf deity, was similar to Egypt's 'Apis', and was believed to control the weather which directly impacted the harvest and prosperity of the nation. They united the two god's ideals and rituals into the one idol made of either solid gold or a wooden carving covered in gold plate to represent the god's image on earth.

'I do understand what Elah is trying to accomplish,' said Tibni in his usual whining tone. 'The people worshipped the Golden Calf before they left Egypt and then in the wilderness while they conquered Canaan, I don't care what they do, but I am not about to begin being religious now.' His small bony fingers grasped his wine cup and he drank greedily sloshing a little of the ruby liquid down his dark beard.

'He is just trying to unite the kingdom under the one ideal or religion.' explained Zimri patiently, placing his own wine mug down on the table as he spoke and leaning back in his chair comfortably. He folded his strong arms over his broad chest casually and stretched his long legs out languidly in front of him.

'I know. That is the only part of his decree I do understand...' Tibni's nasal voice trailed away distractedly as he watched a lovely curvaceous young woman sway her hips seductively while she walked slowly towards their table to refill their empty wine cups.

'Just leave the wine-jug here!' snapped Zimri harshly, irritated that she had managed to take his friends attention away from him for the briefest moment. The woman placed the jug on the table hurriedly and looked at him sullenly, realising that the two men were not going to be prospective clients for the evening. She turned hastily on her heel and walked away still swaying her hips provocatively hoping to entice other interested patrons who would buy her body for the night.

Tibni reluctantly pulled his eyes away from the swaying hypnotic hips and looked back at Zimri's flat expressionless face, he continued where he had left off, 'I think Elah believes that if he unites the kingdom behind this religion, then the people will be afraid of the gods once again and not moan about his own short-comings as much. He can then get away with his negligence and incompetence and just blame the gods for all of his reckless oversights and weak rule and at the same time he avoids having to take the responsibility for any of his failures, addictions and flaws.'

Zimri nodded thoughtfully, his cold black eyes narrowing under thick bushy brows that met in a frown as he agreed with Tibni's astute observation of the king's personal conduct and added to the argument: 'He definitely wants to use the religion for his own gain, to twist the people of Tirzah around his short fat little finger, he wants to gain their support again and manipulate them into paying higher taxes without causing a riot. He would then just use the excuse: That it's not for him, but for the Golden Calf god.' Zimri's voice took on a mocking tone as he mimicked the drunken king. 'The people would become so terrified of upsetting the god that they would do all that Elah demands and more, just to appease some non-existent invisible being into averting whatever disasters could possibly be attributed to the Golden Calf or to this new mystical 'Baal'.'

The wine had been flowing freely and the two men sat together for a long while discussing everything from the day's events to the political situation in Israel all the while drinking the cheap sour wine, they did the same thing most nights. They had been inseparable since childhood, with Tibni always in Zimri's shadow, much smaller in stature and weaker than most men. He was short, skinny, sickly and pale and was not a notable warrior, but preferred to use the subtle art of sly deception and cunning manipulation to accomplish his ends. He was only Zimri's second-in-command because of the dependence the two men had upon one another and was promoted in the army by Zimri who depended upon Tibni's cunning mind and tactical genius, and in return Zimri shielded and protected Tibni with a savage loyalty.

Zimri, by far, the stronger and more dominant of the two, was built like a bear. He was tall and his bulging muscles rippled with every movement he made. He had not yet met an opponent he could not overcome and the men in his squadron were afraid of his brute strength, speed and legendary fighting skills. His bulk was an added advantage because most of the enemies singled him out believing that his massive frame would slow him down in the sword or spear fighting, where speed and agility were crucial. That was what he loved the most, the surprise on their enemies' faces as he parried and lunged with unbelievable grace and unexpected speed that was at odds with his appearance. His feet always seemed to be floating just above the surface of the ground as he moved with elegance and deadly fast accuracy.

He had fiercely protected the weaker more submissive Tibni since childhood, shielding him in all the battles they fought because he realised that with his strength and fighting abilities and Tibni's deviously sly brain, the two made an exceptional team. Their strengths complimenting each other's and cancelling out their weaknesses. In return for Zimri's protection, Tibni became completely subservient to Zimri and hero-worshipped him, obeying all of Zimri's demands, he was totally dependent upon him and Tibni's loyalty and devotion to his friend knew no limits.

There was an element of fear in Tibni too because he understood that they both knew Zimri could completely annihilate him at any moment and because of Zimri's lack of empathy and cold emotionless reason, he would not hesitate to do so if required.

CHAPTER FOUR

Every Friday evening, the people of Tirzah had been commanded by their king to go up to the Golden Calf altar at the high place, instead of celebrating the traditional pass-over meal at their homes with their families which commemorated the end of their enslavement in Egypt.

King Elah had enforced the decree that the people were to no longer allowed to celebrate the pass-over at all which was a constant reminder of the Israelites flight from Egypt during the time of the Exodus led by Moses. He had ordered that the kingdom was to instead worship and honour the god that had brought them to Tirzah, the Golden Calf and to accept the new Phoenician god 'Baal' and his consort 'Ashtoreth', the queen of Heaven.

The altar to the Golden Calf on the high place was built especially for that purpose by Jeroboam, the first king of Israel, after breaking away from the oppressive Davidic dynasty under Rehoboam in Judah. It was situated on the hill to be closer to the god in the sky, with steps down the sides making it easier for the god to descend and be among his subjects if he so desired. The people had been ordered to worship the bull, bringing gifts for the god to buy his favour and blessing, hoping to avert any disasters the god might want to throw their way for his own personal amusement.

Tibni picked his nose and casually inspected the slimy lump of snot on his finger, flicking it away he asked: 'Who gets the gifts, I mean because the gods don't use or need the tribute? It's such a waste of good food, wine and gold!'

'Especially since the nation is experiencing such a severe famine and the extreme poverty everywhere could be averted if the food was distributed to the poor instead.' added Zimri condescendingly.

'Yeah, and no matter how much the people starve, the priests are always so fat and round and the gods don't seem to hear the loud cries of the poor and needy.' argued Tibni in disgust. 'I don't see them changing the poverty of Israel into prosperity.'

Zimri frowned and asked quietly, 'If the gods did really exist, wouldn't they do something about the lack of crops and food in our land or maybe destroy the enemies that Israel is constantly plagued with?'

'You know what I think of the gods...' muttered Tibni angrily gulping greedily from his wine mug. 'It's a joke!' he spat, 'That mad king thinks we will all obediently march off to the high place and worship some golden bull statue or a pole, handing our hard-earned wages over to the priests!'

'I know its bullshit,' snorted Zimri derisively. 'Honestly are we really supposed to believe that there are all these unseen magical beings playing games with us?' he moved his arm in a wide arc around him. 'Have I just waved my arm through the bull?' he laughed sardonically. 'Do these invisible beings really care about us and try to help us by sending us signs and omens? Why would they?' He asked arrogantly, 'they always send signs that could be interpreted in any possible number of ways and because of how it is read, or who reads the omen, it becomes redundant, the reader's own personal desire emerges and not an instruction from these abstract beings. And besides, if they did exist, wouldn't they have more important things to do then play games with us?' Zimri rationalised and his irritation was evident with what he saw as stupid gullible and superstitious people clinging to mystical magic instead of taking the burden of responsibility upon themselves. He was anti-religion but voiced his opinion very carefully and quietly because of the overzealous naïve people around him that did not share his liberal views and would sentence him to death for the chance of earning any of the gods favour and blessings.

The idea of gods and religion amused him; he believed it was all just a means for a handful of priests to control the masses and gain power and riches for themselves. He hated the religious superstitions and believed them to be nothing more than a tool wielded by the priests and the king to exploit the stupid kingdom into doing their will. He didn't believe there were any gods at all, just men pretending, manipulating, influencing and making up stories with fancy rituals and customs to gain an advantage over the susceptible naïve people of the nation.

'Anyone who buys that load of crap is as pathetic as the people selling it to them.' Zimri's icy tone was filled with malevolence. His black eyes twinkled wickedly and the expression on his face was cold, leaving Tibni in no doubt as to his friend's dangerous disposition.

The wine and topic they were discussing was blackening his mood rapidly and he continued in a hushed tone so that Tibni had to listen very carefully to hear properly: 'We are all responsible for our own lives; we don't need some supernatural invisible spirit to guide us to our destiny, lead us to our fate or destroy us. We are just here on our own to make the most of what we have the balls to grasp ourselves, before we die and become dust and disappear from memory forever.' He took a deep breath and sipped his wine slowly as Tibni nodded thoughtfully in agreement.

'The only thing we can hope for is being remembered past the next generation. That is as immortal as it gets…eternity is as long as the future generations remember us for and that is all there is to it! Nothing more, nothing less!' Zimri sneered in a low menacing tone that was filled with ridicule as he continued, 'These priests are trying to sell a non-existent eternity for food, wine, gold, power and influence and they make me sick! They are exploiting the poor!' He slammed his wine cup on the table angrily emphasising his point and the ceramic shattered in his big hand. He and sat back quickly in his chair and examined the deep bleeding cut in the palm of his hand where a sharp shard of the cup had sliced through his thick calloused skin. He looked around and realised that he had drawn too much unwanted attention to the two of them and smiled charmingly at the other patrons in silent apology as Zimri signalled to the half-naked serving girl to bring him another cup.

'Maybe we hit the luck and King Elah drops dead suddenly.' announced Tibni cheerfully, quickly changing the subject and turning it back to what they believed was the root cause of Israel's misfortune. He was subtly trying to plant the seeds of an idea into Zimri's massive head.

'All that will do is put some other idiot on the throne,' answered Zimri dejectedly looking around him at the people inside the brothel. The silence stretched out between the two friends and then Zimri looked up suddenly and said, 'But then maybe a stronger king could pull the kingdom back from the pit of disgrace it is currently in, back to its former glory that was achieved under King Baasha or even King Jeroboam.' His voice had become filled with a small amount of hope as he finished his sentence and his black eyes gleamed with an evil determination.

'Do you think Elah is so weak as to hand our kingdom over to another country?' inquired Tibni cunningly, he had been worrying about that particular issue for a while now and needed to hear Zimri's opinion on the matter as well as attempt to mobilise his friend into some kind of action. He knew he was the brains and not the brawn in the partnership, but if he could convince Zimri to kill Elah, he would be able to rule the kingdom alongside his friend, through his friend to a certain extent, and the possibilities were endless. Tibni smiled shrewdly as he waited for Zimri's reply, he just had to set his scheme in motion by carefully using Zimri in an ingenious way to eliminate the only obstacle between them and absolute power, King Elah.

'He seems to be adopting the culture and superstitions of Phoenicia lately.' replied Zimri seriously while gazing thoughtfully around the room, as another scantily dressed woman brought them a fresh wine jug and poured him a fresh cup of the sour wine while she smiled seductively at him. She too was hoping to attract his attention long enough to seduce him but recoiled quickly and hurried away when she saw the evil malice in Zimri's cold soulless black eyes.

CHAPTER FIVE

There was a fascinating fancy new pole recently erected in the centre of the city, it was called an Ashtoreth pole and the people were expected to worship at it too, bringing gifts of grain and wine, as well as anything else they wanted to sacrifice to the goddess. Worship included many ritual sexual acts as Ashtoreth was the goddess of fertility.

The wooden pole stood straight up and represented the fully erect male reproductive organ. It was skilfully carved and stood taller than the buildings surrounding it, it had vines growing at the base twining upwards around it decoratively, the vines were also supposed to symbolise prosperity and bountiful harvests of the land, while the pole symbolised plentiful human reproduction.

There were rumours that the Phoenician traveller who had arrived at the palace was behind the mysterious new pole and had quickly installed himself at the gullible King Elah's side. The spies in the palace had reported to Zimri that he was a high priest of Sidon, which was a province of Phoenicia and that the new religion was to do with Baal worship. Some said the Ashtoreth pole had something to do with Baal's consort, the queen of Heaven and was a representation of the fertility goddess and associated with the stars, Ashtoreth was often represented by the moon too, because the queen shone slightly less brightly then Baal who was frequently combined with the worship of the sun.

It was rather exciting for the citizens because the many rituals to this 'queen of heaven' included several types of sexual ceremonies for the aiding of fertility amongst the people, livestock and crops in the fields, and the citizens of Tirzah were eager to adopt the goddess because it gave them a free religious licence to have as many sexual affairs as often as they wanted to. The act of sex itself was seen as an act of worshipping the goddess. Suddenly all the people were eager to become pious, devout followers at the Ashtoreth pole. The uniting of men with women and men with men in the sex act was said to bring good favour and blessings from the 'queen of Heaven' as well as gain them an audience with her to petition their personal requests.

The previous week many of the citizens were in an uproar because a new-born baby girl had been sacrificed at the pole to the goddess. The people involved claimed that it was what the goddess had demanded to bring about an end to the famine in the entire land.

Zimri wasn't bothered about the death of the baby and didn't care as long as he was unaffected by it, but he was truly concerned that if a mother could be convinced to give her only child to the fire to satisfy some new mysterious mystical belief in a previously unknown goddess, then what wouldn't she do? What more would she hold back when she had already given her most precious possession, her own flesh and blood to a non-existent, fictional being?

The Phoenician high priest worried both Zimri and Tibni because the King was so easily fooled and far too gullible, 'I'm scared that this Phoenician gets his hooks too deeply into Elah and makes him a puppet and we end up dancing to his tune,' Zimri confessed leaning forward and placing his hands flat on the table either side of his wine cup, 'Our useless king is so willingly misled and too damned easy to deceive, Israel could then become a target ripe for hostile invasion and then our income would go to a foreign king instead of into Elah's stomach.' murmured Zimri seriously, checking around him to see that no one was listening to their treasonous conversation.

'I've heard his name is Eth-Baal,' stated Tibni in a matter of fact tone. 'Do you think it's his actual name or a general name for his position – you know, like Pharaoh isn't the man's name but his position - what he is?'

'I'm not sure,' mused Zimri slowly, lost in thought, a few silent moments passed and then he added quietly with his voice dangerously low, 'I think we need to keep a very close eye on this odd Phoenician, he is a serious threat and needs eliminating quickly.'

Zirmi stroked his short dark pointed beard broodingly for a while and stared off into the distance, his dead black eyes staring blankly, giving his face a dark vacant and poisonous appearance. Thoughts swirled around his head for what felt like a very long time, and then suddenly snapping back into focus he announced: 'I've had a few spies in the employ of the palace staff watching him for a while now and they say he behaves very suspiciously and some even tell me that he claims to be the king of Sidon, but he came here without an entourage or any kind of evidence of his position.' Zimri's face was an unreadable mask, giving no clue to his dangerous thoughts as he pondered the mysterious circumstances surrounding the high priest slash king from Phoenicia and analysed all the information he had acquired. He was unable to figure out what or who this Phoenician was because everything that the man had done to that point was an enigma and contradicted much of the etiquette and customs that they were accustomed too.

Tibni watched his friend intently and couldn't help wondering if there was going to be another sudden and unexplained disappearance from Tirzah, there had been countless over the years, men, women and even children. He added a little more fuel to the already smouldering fire making it even more tempting for Zimri to act. 'Do you really think he's here scouting from Phoenicia?' he asked artfully, his small beady eyes adopting a fake innocence that appeared ridiculous in his weasel-like pointy face. After a long drawn out silence, Zimri replied thoughtfully, 'Yes, I do... and he conveniently arrived here shortly after the army left for Philistia four months ago.'

Tibni continued smoothly baiting Zimri slyly and airing his own concerns at the same time; 'If he is doing any covert reconnaissance, then we are in really hot water already. The high priest has access to everything and anyone, there's no limit to the damage that he could inflict upon us!'

'I think we need to take action to protect Israel immediately.' said Zimri suddenly in a flat frightening tone. 'I know from my spies that he goes to the pole each evening to lead the worship there, he seems to enjoy the sexual rituals very much and performs them with a different man or woman daily. It would be almost too easy to arrange his disappearance…we could make it look like he was attacked by wild animals outside of the city.' Zimri was suddenly aware he was speaking out loud and looked at Tibni coldly; he knew he had his friend's complete loyalty and could convince Tibni that it was for the good of the nation, but he needn't have worried, Tibni was staring at him with eagerness and satisfaction written plainly all over his calculating face.

'I've done it!' thought Tibni triumphantly, elated that his carefully planted words had taken root and grown into the idea in Zimri's head and had mobilised him into taking immediate violent action.

'If we leave now, he should be just finishing up his sexual service and then we could grab him on his way back into the palace!' suggested Tibni enthusiastically. 'He doesn't ever have any bodyguards or soldiers with him.'

Zimri dipped his head very slightly and finished his friends thought, 'The city gates are still going to be open for a while and it's the change of the guards soon. While the men are swopping posts, we can easily slip out of the city unseen and we can get him out into the wilderness, with plenty of blood, his body should attract a wolf or bear, even a lion if we are very lucky, then there will be no questions regarding his disappearance and we can discredit his mysterious Baal or this strange queen of heaven for not protecting him properly.' declared Zimri with a cold deadly determination that sent a terrible shiver down Tibni's spine and he couldn't help but notice the wicked sparkle in Zimri's excited eyes as he explained the plan.

Tibni spat a large yellow blob of phlegm onto the ground next to where he sat and Zimri smiled an evil malicious smile as he stood to leave. 'Let's go,' he ordered quietly, making the decision instantly, 'Act normally, and don't forget to squeeze your favourite whore's ass on the way out. We need to look like we do every night.'

'Right,' said Tibni and gave a mock salute placing his stained ceramic wine cup carefully down on the crude wooden table that was so sticky and discoloured from the copious amounts of spilt wine and covered in layers of grime. He pushed his chair back and it scraped loudly on the hard packed earthen floor covered in smelly damp rotting straw. He stood feeling slightly unsteady and waited a few moments for the light-headedness to pass. He looked around him to see if anyone was watching them, and satisfied, he followed Zimri towards the door.

The smell of stale wine and urine along with the stench of unwashed bodies, musty sweat and rotting straw on the floor was thick in the air and the men in the brothel were either too drunk to notice them leaving a little earlier than usual, or they were too preoccupied with the prostitutes draped seductively over them practising their age-old craft.

Outside, the fresh air was helping to sober Tibni up, and he lifted his face to the breeze blowing gently from the east and closed his eyes enjoying the cool refreshing caress on his face. He gulped in a few slow deep breaths and began feeling his head clear like a rag sweeping away the cobwebs in a dusty room.

CHAPTER SIX

They began walking together towards the centre of the city. A few of the guards on duty saw them and saluted their senior officers as they passed by them, they were amused that their commander was out and enjoying the wine and relaxed atmosphere around the town. Zimri greeted his men cheerfully by name with his arm draped casually around Tibni's narrow shoulders. They swayed together as they walked, stumbling every so often because of the profuse amounts of the cheap sour wine they had consumed and Zimri silently cursed himself for drinking so much.

'We must not attract any attention at all,' he whispered quietly in Tibni's ear, 'Elah loves this guy enough to have us both put to the sword or worse, for what we are talking about now.' He looked around him again to make certain no one was paying any attention to them and they were not being followed. It was a habit ingrained into him because of his hunting…his natural predatory skills; his ability to stalk his prey undetected and then snatch a victim without being caught. It took plenty of planning and practice to get away with all he had done and Zimri had mastered the art of stealthily stalking to perfection.

The pole loomed up ahead and they saw the people gathered around it but there was no sign of the high priest. 'Where is he?' asked Tibni suddenly disappointed that the plan was in danger of being rescheduled, or worse, called off completely, he was eager to please his friend, knowing that Zimri wanted, or rather, needed blood…and it would safe-guard the nation for the immediate future.

'I don't see him,' growled Zimri darkly as they approached the crowd gathered around the pole. People were pouring oil and wine out at the foot of the wooden pole, making a sticky oily mud bath around the phallic looking object where the vines were planted.

Zimri looked to his left and saw that a woman was convulsing violently on the floor near to where Tibni stood. He watched her in disgusted fascination. She was foaming at the mouth and her eyes were rolled completely back in their sockets making them look like creamy white round pearls in her deathly pale face. Her tunic was soaked with sweat and frothy spit and ripped open down the front; her sagging breasts were flopping about pathetically as she shook and shuddered on the ground. The stench of urine coming from her was overpowering, and the dust and sand was forming a sticky thick paste on the wet patches of her tunic and all over her legs. Her bare feet were kicking weakly and strange choking sounds where coming from her thinly stretched lips.

Zimri stepped closer to her and kicked her viciously, 'What the hell is this?' he asked in disgust as his sandal met the flesh of her back, watching the woman writhe uncontrollably was frightening and fascinating to him all at once.

He looked up from the pitiful, jerking female flesh and spotted one of his little spies approaching them; he had a grubby sack-cloth tunic on and was only about ten years old. His face was filthy and caked in layers of dirt and grime; it appeared he had not bathed in months. He looked like he had not eaten a decent meal in weeks, his cheek bones stood out prominently on his skeletal face. 'Master, the priest you said I must watch is gone,' the child spoke with a soft high voice and scratched absently at the lice in his matted greasy hair. 'He left this morning. No one has seen him since then.' The child held his thin bony hand out as he spoke waiting for his payment and Zimri dropped a small coin into his fingers. The scrawny boy scampered away on painfully thin legs that looked like they would snap like twigs at any moment, with his prize clutched tightly in his skinny hand to get something to eat before the coin was either stolen or taken away forcibly by his starving mother.

'Dammit!' exclaimed Zimri fiercely; his face was cold and impassive as he looked around him. The people all wore tatty tunics, no more than filthy rags; they were tired and hungry and looked so pathetic and pitiful that it disgusted Zimri and filled him with a renewed fiery rage. 'Weak people wallowing in a weak city ruled by a weak king!' He thought with violent loathing.

The buildings in the centre of the city were run down and were in desperate need of maintenance and repairs. The houses were crammed in so closely together causing a serious fire hazard and breeding disease and filth. There was plenty evidence of rat infestation everywhere they looked and the citizens didn't seem to notice, they were beyond the point of caring. The entire scene was shockingly bleak, despicable and disgraceful.

The noise too was overwhelming as the citizens prayed and chanted creating a loud buzzing racket of indecipherable sound, the people slashed themselves with blades as they cried out, offering their own blood to appease and invoke this foreign Baal to provide food for them. Zimri felt the bile rise in his throat and turned away quickly before anyone saw the revulsion on his face. It was this pathetic bunch of humanity that he was supposed to risk his life for each time the army went to fight an enemy, and he was repulsed, disgusted and sickened by what he saw.

The taxes had been raised yet again and the people of Israel were struggling to make ends meet. Desperate for food many of the women were turning to prostitution, even selling their own children if they could. There were beggars everywhere crying out for food or help of any kind and a few young boys sold their bodies to the older men who preferred the unnatural perverse pleasure of sodomy, just to survive for one more day, one more meal.

'This is a classic case of the fat cat getting fatter while the poor are getting poorer.' sighed Tibni gloomily, feeling the weight of the oppression of the poor people crushing his spirits as he looked around him.

Even more outrageous was the fact that the king was never sober, his nickname around town, whispered behind hands mockingly, and laughed at in groups was 'The King Wine Skin'.

All the people of Israel hated him and his oppressive rule and blamed his shameless drinking and debauchery for the failings of the kingdom, but Elah didn't seem to notice or even care, he just drank and partied and ordered new fancy purple robes, made in fine Egyptian linen and dyed in the extremely rare Phoenician purple dye, to fit his ever expanding obese waistline.

From what Zimri could understand of the ritual he was witnessing at the Ashtoreth pole, it seemed that Baal was the god of weather and the people were asking for rain and a good harvest to feed everyone in the city, and bring prosperity through the exporting of the surplus to the surrounding regions.

Rage continued to swell in him and he welcomed the feeling, allowing it to wash through him, to power him with its white hot intensity, loving the hatred he felt and allowing it to carry him along on its fast flowing current like a river rushing towards the sea. His hatred for the king and the fury that boiled within him fuelling an idea and he dwelt on the thoughts, directing the flow of his anger into a plan...

'We live to fight another day.' said Tibni clapping Zimri casually on the shoulder and startling him from the dark thoughts suddenly as he spoke the words they always said to one another after they had survived another battle.

'Yes, fight another day!' intoned Zimri dully turning to leave and head back towards the barracks; he stopped and turned back to Tibni suddenly and said inquiringly: 'You coming?'

Tibni nodded and joined Zimri and together they walked dejectedly back along the deserted streets towards the brothel to continue their drinking. The discussion turned once more to the present poverty stricken state of the nation and they reminisced on the past glories of Israel.

CHAPTER SEVEN

'Kingdoms should not go to the sons of kings just because they are born to a king,' mumbled Tibni drunkenly, they had sat down again at the same table they had vacated before going to find the Phoenician and having the plan to kill him thwarted by his sudden disappearance. 'What makes Elah worthy of sovereignty? Just that he was sired by an unfortunate spilling of the great Baasha's seed?' Tibni probed recklessly, his voice dripped with sulky disrespect and disappointment. 'The strongest person with the best possible capabilities and leadership skills should be the king.' he continued and told Zimri that he thought King Baasha, the current King Elah's father, had been a very capable and skilled ruler 'It just emphasises Elah's weaknesses in contrast to the glory of King Baasha, and all his great accomplishments. Elah's uselessness is in stark disparity to his father's effectiveness.' Tibni was extremely discouraged and the scorn he felt was evident in his treasonous tone as he continued: 'He is just so weak and pathetic like a spoilt fat baby, the total and complete opposite of his revered father.'

'I agree,' responded Zimri quietly and then added: 'Baasha assassinated the King Nadab, the son of King Jeroboam. That took some balls!' his eyes sparkled with the admiration he felt as he spoke, 'Jeroboam was the very first king of Israel's ten northern tribes and he was strong and really remarkable at ruling this kingdom. He broke the ten tribes away from the oppressive yoke of King Solomon's spoilt son Rehoboam, splitting the kingdom and seizing the larger portion for himself-this throne.' His arm swept in a wide arc indicating the area around him and the reverence in

Zimri's voice was obvious, he respected a person who took what they wanted and let nothing stand in their way.

'Our nation is so young, but in the short time it has existed, it has been filled with blood and strong men.' said Tibni, enjoying the camaraderie and conversation. His eyes were glazed from the wine he was steadily consuming.

'I agree with you,' countered Zimri lightly, they loved discussing the former glories of Israel and wishing for them to become a reality once more, it was their favourite subject. 'King Solomon was very wise and a very great king to the United Kingdom, he brought wealth and prosperity to us all, it's just a pity that his son was also so spoilt and arrogant. Just like…Argh!' Zimri exclaimed in disgust and in his irritation, he swiped his earthenware cup off the table. It bounced over the straw covered hard packed earth and shattered into large fragments in front of a pretty serving girl who looked up at him in fearful surprise. She smiled sweetly as she bent down casually and picked up the broken pieces of the pottery, making sure that one of her ample breasts drooped temptingly out of her loosely fitted robe. She took it over to a bowl at the back of the room and casually dropped the fragments into it, all the while moving with practiced slow seduction, before going and getting another cup from behind the counter and bringing over it to him.

Zimri snatched it from her hand roughly, his menacing stare meeting her smiling eyes and immediately her expression turned to shocked terror bringing a sadistic smile to Zimri's face. She moved away quickly and looked over her shoulder at the two men with naked fear in her eyes.

Zimri filled his new cup as he spoke, 'Solomon's son Rehoboam was selfish and had cared nothing for the people of Israel, if he only had cared a little less about his expensive fancy robes and gold filled palaces, then Jeroboam would not have been able to wrest the ten tribes away from him. Rehoboam is another good example of a spoilt weak and negligent son following a great and powerful father, the son that brings the glory and gold that the father fiercely fought for to nothing but dung and ashes.' Zimri stared pensively into his once more empty wine cup and placed it in front of Tibni smoothly, waiting for the other man to finish his drink.

Tibni gulped the last of his wine dregs down and shuddered at the bitter taste; he refilled their cups again and signalled to a girl to bring another fresh jug of wine. 'Can you imagine ruling the combined kingdom, the whole twelve tribes of Israel? He asked, 'and that only about a mere fifty years ago, it was a reality?' Tibni's voice stumbled over the words as the wine he had drunk dulled his senses.

'I can,' answered Zimri, 'It just needs a strong capable man to unite the two kingdoms again and rule them with an iron fist!' he slammed his fist down on the table making it wobble precariously and the cups bounced noisily slopping their contents over the edges onto the already sticky wooden surface.

Zimri continued to elaborate: 'Strength is the only way to bring the glory and splendour and wisdom that made King Solomon so great, back to this kingdom! It's definitely possible, we just need to rid the nation of the weak cowardly parasite of a king that we have now.'

Zimri's face was unemotional and unreadable as he spoke, his arms were folded over his barrel chest and his eyes were narrowed and constantly scanning the dimly lit room. 'King Jeroboam was strong and ruled for twenty-two very prosperous years. He built us the shrines for the Golden Calf worship at Dan and Bethel to prevent the weak and superstitious citizens from going back over to Rehoboam in Jerusalem so that they could worship in Solomon's temple there. He made this city his capital. He fought the Egyptians, who had given him refuge when Solomon had tried to have him killed, but who then had turned on him suddenly asking him for tribute when he became our first king.

Pharaoh Shishak the first, had led his troops from Egypt and Cush and invaded us when Jeroboam had refused to buy his throne from the jumped up, self-indulgent Egyptian who had no right to ask us for tribute of any kind. Jeroboam then pushed the Egyptians back and sent them running home and gave us our first taste of national pride, dignity and prosperity. He pulled us together and this nation was forged! That was a man who knew what he wanted and he made Israel a name to be reckoned with!' Zimri could not keep the admiration from his voice as he spoke about one of his hero's accomplishments, he winked at the scared prostitute who was watching him like a mouse would watch a dangerous snake, and he held his cup out to Tibni for yet another refill, to which Tibni happily complied.

Zimri drained his cup in one long drink, gulping the red sour liquid down and placing his cup back on the table, he covered it with his hand to prevent it from being topped up again. He knew his limits and didn't want any more of the addictive alcoholic beverage.

Tibni filled his own cup liberally and added: 'Jeroboam's son Nadab was also weak like Rehoboam in Judah, and he was not worthy of being a king. Baasha assassinated him during a siege just like this one happening right now at Gibbethon, and he seized the throne twenty-six years ago, pulling Israel back from the down-ward spiral it had begun to experience under the short two-year reign of Nadab.' Tibni knew he was taking a huge risk but continued anyway, still planting the seeds in Zimri's mind that was such rich and fertile ground for the idea to take root in and grow into action.

'If you look at our history, every time a weak, useless son succeeds a great king, the son winds up dead...' Zimri observed, his voice was flat and emotionless, and Tibni thought happily to himself that he was succeeding to lure Zimri into the idea of killing Elah and claiming the throne for himself. He had to manoeuvre carefully in this situation that he was trying to create with Zimri, without alerting him too soon for fear of angering him and having to contend with his terrible and deadly wrath. He wanted it to seem like Zimri's idea, he didn't want Zimri to realise he was being baited and manipulated into doing anything.

CHAPTER EIGHT

Baasha was the commander of Israel's armed forces under King Nadab before he snatched the throne away in the brutal, bloody murder of the king. He had then ruled for twenty-four years with an iron fist, he was feared by his enemies and his subjects, they had respected him and his only mistake in the two men's opinion was having only the one stupid son in his line to inherit his throne when he died.

The nation had mourned the sudden and unexpected death of their king for an entire thirty days; with much wailing and fasting out of respect for who he was and what he had accomplished. Everyone across the kingdom had worn sackcloth and ashes and the men had all shaved their beards off in anguish and mourning. King Baasha had been a good leader and had done a great deal for the furtherance of the kingdom of Israel.

Throughout his reign, Baasha had kept the Southern Kingdom of Judah at bay with his fortifications of Ramah to prevent the Judahites from entering or leaving the city, restricting their trade and weakening the long term enemy of Israel's economy considerably.

It was only when King Asa of Judah had appealed for support from Israel's own ally, Ben-Hadad of Assyria, and had bribed him in huge amounts of gold and tribute, that the backstabbing, unreliable Ben-Hadad had then marched his army against Tirzah. Baasha was forced to withdraw his troops and defend the land of Israel from the Assyrian invaders. Unfortunately, Baasha had been beaten and was forced to abandon his fortifications of Ramah for good.

'Baasha only lost that war because he was deceived by Ben-Hadad and King Asa.' muttered Tibni sullenly, he gazed into the distance and added, 'He was doing a great thing, if the two-faced Ben-Hadad had not been bought over to Asa's side by bribery, then we would have brought Judah to their knees into submission to us and united the two kingdoms a long time ago and Ramah would then have been our kingdom's capital.'

Some of the men looked over at their two most senior officers deep in conversation and nodded in agreement at what they heard. King Baasha had inspired them all and had gained their loyalty but none of them could find it in them to serve his son with the same respect, devotion and discipline.

Zimri thought of Baasha as one of his role-models, he saw a lot of the former army commander and self-made king in himself. 'If he could do it and succeed, then so can I.' he announced quietly to Tibni who smiled slyly in agreement, Zimri was very drunk and he stood to leave, swaying slightly he bid his friend goodnight and staggered out the door into the fresh night air.

Walking to his officer's quarters next to the barracks for the lower ranking men, Zimri thought about the conversation he had just had and the plan that had begun as a tiny seed of malcontent became a flower and bloomed in his mind. He was cheerful as he arrived at his room and began his daily routine of cleaning his armour ready for the following day filled with anticipation for the future. 'History repeats itself,' he mused softly, 'after two years of weak rule, Nadab was assassinated by an army commander who became a great king, Baasha was and is still renowned. Now, the wheel has turned once again and Israel has once more been under a weak king's rule for two years, and during a siege just like the one Baasha took advantage of, I'll make my move, and once again, a commander of the army will rule the kingdom and usher in a new and great era.'

He was lost in thought as he sharpened his sword and his dagger. The ritual was significant to Zimri, giving him enormous satisfaction and comfort. The movement of whetstone and blade, working against one another to make the metal razor sharp was soothing. Knowing that the hidden dagger was always ready and within reach in his belt under his robes was a large part of his confidence. He had killed many people with his secret hidden blade, people who had gotten in his way or disagreed with him or even just because he wanted to shed some blood at that very moment.

The dagger was special to him; it was a trophy from his childhood. He had acquired it from an Egyptian merchant he had murdered when he was a very young boy. He had been approached by the merchant who had wanted to pay him for sex and Zimri had played along, following the Egyptian to a dark back alleyway and then when the man was out of sight from the street, he had attacked him with a stone thrown hard, hitting the back of the Egyptian's head. The man immediately fell down unconscious to the ground and Zimri had quickly searched his robes and found the dagger, he had used it to slit the Egyptians throat and kept the dagger as well as the purse full of gold coins he had found on the body.

The blade was beautifully worked with a pommel that was richly jewelled with blood red rubies and sparkling diamonds. Immediately the rubies had been very symbolic to Zimri as they reminded him of splattered blood droplets and the dagger had felt so natural in his hand, as if it was moulded for him alone. He had not been without it ever since that day many years ago. It had quickly become his secret weapon, very few people knew that he even carried it constantly concealed beneath his robes.

He knew he could and did kill with his bare hands often, but the dagger gave him the release of seeing life giving blood flow away from his victim, something slightly more difficult when he had only his hands as weapons. The two blades gave him a rewarding release he couldn't put into words, he felt aroused whenever he watched his blade penetrate the flesh of his victim, it was almost a substitute for sexual pleasure. He could not remember how many people had spilled their blood on both of his trophy blades and he loved the agonized surprise on their faces when he had suddenly and unexpectedly slashed at their throats or stabbed them fatally – strangers, friends, enemies and even rivals in the army, absolutely anyone who got in his way.

CHAPTER NINE

He'd almost been caught once; years ago after he had begun giving in to the dark temptations inside him that were awoken when he had first killed the Egyptian merchant. He was green then and very unsure of his evil lusts and he had had to perfect his hunting skills over time with much experimentation and practice. The memory gave him cause to smile to himself as he relived the time he had killed the young girl in the street at sundown.

She was young-twelve maybe thirteen, and was returning home alone from the field where she had been working during the day as a labourer. Zimri was only a lowly soldier then and was stationed with his garrison just outside the city of Ramah. 'Gods, she was gorgeous,' he sighed, he had seen her and wanted her immediately…not like normal men want a girl…he had wanted to possess her completely, he needed to absorb her vitality and possess her entirely, to be the last image she ever saw. He had wanted her lifeblood to flow for him alone, to watch her essence leave her body…slowly, to capture her spirit and make her soul belong to him forever. She had been his favourite, his first young girl, the first of many.

Zimri remembered the entire event like it had just happened, he relived the incident over and over again and he was always trying to recreate the rush and sexual release he had felt when her steaming hot blood had bubbled from her throat all down her tunic and over his hand covering them both in the rich ruby red liquid. He had held her close and looked deep into her beautiful soft brown eyes as her spirit left the shell of her body slowly;

knowing that she would forever be a part of him, belonging to him completely and he had been so powerfully aroused that he was utterly intoxicated in the moment and unaware of anything else going on around him.

He had inhaled her last frothy breath as it burst from her ruined throat, savouring the metallic tinge in the air and felt her heart beat against him weaken and fade until it eventually stilled. The satisfaction was indescribable, he could not find the words to explain the hypnotic sensations that he had felt that night, and he wanted to feel that way again. He never gave up trying to recapture the enchanting release that seemed to just elude him from that delightful night onwards.

Her young firm body had gone limp and he was standing still holding her tightly against him in an embrace of death, prolonging his pleasure, dragging out the moment of ecstasy, staring into her upturned lifeless brown eyes, so utterly absorbed in his complete arousal that he had not heard the small group of his detachment approaching. Tibni was with three other soldiers from his unit and they had almost walked right into Zimri. Tibni had seen him and the girl and had smoothly diverted the men away down a nearby alleyway while loudly calling out to Zimri in a taunting tone that he should get some privacy if he was going to bed the local girls.

Zimri still wondered to this day if Tibni had seen what was really happening there or if he just saw Zimri and assumed he was enjoying innocent sexual pleasures with the girl, it had been very dark, there was no moon that night and the shadows would have concealed much of the truth of the situation and Tibni might not have seen the dark patches of the spilled blood.

Zimri grinned maliciously to himself and put his blade under his straw mattress for the night, he tidied his room as he thought that Tibni had never mentioned that incident again after nearly ten years, so he didn't think Tibni knew or suspected the real truth about him, who or what he really was...and if he did, he was wise enough to keep his mouth tightly shut.

He had overcome numerous obstacles in his life to get to where he now was. Coming from a very poor family, Zimri could not remember his mother at all, she had died when he was very young, abandoning him to a vicious, merciless father who beat him without cause and punished him without reason. The man was sadistic and loved humiliating the young Zimri publically and physically hurting him periodically, once when Zimri was eight years old; his father had tied him to a post in a pig sty.

Pigs were believed to be one of the vilest, most unclean creatures on the earth and totally forbidden and avoided in their culture. They were not even farmed at all by the Israelites and being tied-up in their pen on a Gentile farm outside of the territory of Israel was the most severe insult and worst public humiliation imaginable to any Israelite.

He never knew exactly what his crime had been to deserve that severe punishment, and the old man had never told him, not even on his death-bed a few years later was Zimri enlightened to his wrongdoing.

The filthy animals had snorted at his tunic and Zimri had kicked out wildly every time one of the unclean beasts had come near to him. The two days and nights in the Gentile's farmyard just outside of Moab, had been one of Zimri's worst memories and he still had occasional nightmares about the pigs snorting and squealing, grunting and nuzzling at his legs.

Zimri had hated his father, but the hatred burnt inside him like a white hot flame, burning all traces of weakness away. Pushing him to excellence and powering him to greatness, motivating him to achieve success against all the odds. He wanted…he wanted to prove to the man that he was a worthy son and punish his father in every way possible to make him sorry for being such a terrible abusive parent to him as a young boy.

To make his father pay, he had to show the old man that he was not the good for nothing waste of life his father claimed that he was, but instead, the successful, fearless warrior that his unit respected and admired.

He excelled in the army ranks quickly after proving himself time and again on the battle field in the infantry, he loved the fighting and the bloodiness of battle as it was another form of release for him.

He had learned to ride horses quickly and loved the freedom he experienced while riding, the feeling of flying above the ground at high speed and controlling a powerful beast gave him such a thrill. He had excelled quickly on horseback and had been allowed to join the junior charioteers after he was stationed at Ramah, he achieved the rank of commander of half the chariot force within a few years after he had mastered the art of the chariot and murdered the useless man in the position he coveted at the time, opening it up for himself.

He felt that he was held back only by his arch-enemy, Omri who was in the same rank as he was at that time and then in a deceitful, underhanded move – he was cheated, and Omri had been promoted to general of the army instead of him!

CHAPTER TEN

Zimri had many eyes and ears in Israel, having set up a network of loyal supporters to spy for him when he had begun moving up in the ranks of the army. He used his spies to gather information about anything that could be of use to him in his career or any other possible way now or in the future.

The little spies, or rats as he referred to them, were also useful when he wanted to plant information about someone or something, or spread vicious rumours, or even plant the seeds of doubt in the city amongst the citizens, as long as there was someone listening to or spreading rumours, Zimri knew about it almost immediately.

Anything from the nation's enemies to political movements within Tirzah was reported back to him quickly through his spy network. It was often said that Zimri knew what the king of Judah, miles away to the south, had eaten for breakfast or when the Pharaoh farted in Egypt.

He had suggested what he thought was a brilliant idea to the king before the siege had begun; a system of spies was to enter Gibbethon under the guise of traders and vendors to spread fear amongst the citizens with rumours of the Israelites battle prowess and deadly skills and gain information on the Philistines condition and military strategy.

The information they could gather on the enemy's weaponry, and circumstances inside the city would then get back out to them and would be vital to the Israelite army.

At that time, the Philistines had very sophisticated weaponry made from a new stronger material that was far superior to that of any of the other surrounding nations, and the Israelites were desperate to learn their weapon manufacturing techniques and then duplicate it, if not improve on their designs and gain an added advantage.

Zimri believed that knowledge was power and information would help them strike a quick and fatal blow to the Philistines. The senseless King Elah had given all the credit once again to Omri, and Omri had just accepted all the honour and praise without correcting the pathetic king! 'Another fool to be dealt with when I get the opportunity,' he thought broodingly, the list was growing steadily longer.

Only a month before the siege had begun, the Philistines had raided a small village outside of Tirzah and killed twenty-seven of Zimri's men during the attack. The Israelite soldiers had fought bravely and fiercely. The fighting had been brutal, bloody and savage; the Philistines had surrounded the village and were riding between the houses setting them all on fire. Torching whatever would burn, destroying crops and rounding up the livestock to take back to Gibbethon with them.

Screaming could be heard coming from all directions as women were raped and mutilated. Civilian men from the village were lying dead and scattered about everywhere, they had courageously, but foolishly tried to repel to the Philistines and defend their women and children inside the village. Children had been knocked down and trampled by the horses as they had tried to run away and hide.

Some of the Philistine raiders had begun a sport of throwing small babies high into the air and letting them fall to their deaths as they hit the ground with a loud wet thud, their heads bursting open on impact like over-ripe watermelons. One of the Philistines had thrown a baby boy up in the air and then caught the infant on his spear laughing as the impaled baby wailed weakly, dying slowly.

The carnage was terrible. There were swarms of flies everywhere and flocks of carrion birds and stray dogs were attacking the corpses left unattended, taking scraps of flesh with them as they were continuously driven away in a futile attempt to return some dignity to the Israelite dead until they could be buried.

Zimri's warriors had arrived at the village and slain most of the raiders in a quick and sudden surprise attack, only a handful of the enemy had escaped. Omri and his men had arrived a little later, and because his men and horses were fresher and not tired from the battle, they were able to ride faster and catch up to the escaping raiders executing them all, not one Philistine escaped with his life that day. They were hung from trees outside the village as a warning and a message to other would be raiders in the region.

King Elah had never even bothered to ask why Zimri's men had arrived at the village before Omri and his unit did, a good king would have noticed that crucial detail, but Elah had his head so far up Omri's arse that he couldn't see for all the shit in his eyes. Zimri's anger burned brightly once more when he thought about that injustice. 'That alone should have proved that I would have been a better general then Omri!' he fumed to himself.

The raids from Gibbethon in Philistia were becoming more and more frequent and deadly, each time the Philistines attacked a defenceless Israelite village, never a fortified city with high strong walls, but always an open farming community surrounded only by fields of crops and orchards, quick and easy, accessible targets, the Philistines were becoming bolder and more vicious with each deadly attack.

The Moabites were often sending out scouts too and would have to be dealt with quickly before they saw a weakness and attacked Israel. The kingdom of Judah was a constant worry, needing to be taught that they couldn't just exploit the farmers and rural villages along the border of Israel, but while the king was too weak and drunk to act, the people of Israel were permanently harassed and suffered for it.

Thinking about how he had been cheated and how the promotion to general was stolen from him unjustly was what decided the matter for Zimri. 'I will show them all! Baasha had the right idea, I will take the throne!' he decided firmly and settled into bed comfortably. Once his decision was made, sleep came easily and he awoke the next morning feeling refreshed and eager for the day ahead.

CHAPTER ELEVEN

Tibni caught up to Zimri leaving the parade ground early the next morning. He had completed the routine roll-call of his men and the shift changes were finalized for the day and he was just finishing off with the debriefings from the previous night's watchmen when Tibni spoke softly in his ear: 'I just want to say that I'm behind you, my friend, you know that right?' Tibni whispered earnestly, 'I mean, about what we discussed last night, assassinations and kings worthy of their thrones...' he let the statement hang in the air for a moment before adding, 'I think you would make a terrific king. Just don't forget me when you get to the top.' he added winking and smiling at Zimri as they walked along the corridor towards their next duty together.

'Don't ever give me reason to.' snapped Zimri menacingly, his icy-black eyes flicking quickly with irritation. He needed Tibni as an ally, he was someone who could be used to achieve an objective, expendable if necessary, but useful for the moment. 'You know that I have always rewarded loyalty and brave service without question before, there will be a general's position opening up soon if you're interested.' Zimri spoke smoothly, cleverly dangling the carrot before his friends face as a powerful incentive.

They reached the throne room and Zimri walked straight past the men standing guard at the beautifully carved heavy gold plated doors. They saluted him smartly and he acknowledged their greeting with a slight incline of his head. His ranking gave him access to anywhere in the city and the palace, only the king's bed chambers were off-limits to him along with everyone in the palace

41

except for the king's chamber maids and when invited, his wives and concubines.

The two men walked towards the throne and knelt knowing before Zimri even looked up at the ornately carved wooden chair that was beautifully inlaid with gold, that it would be vacant for the rest of that day, the Chamberlain, Zimri knew, would be absent too. The Seneschal looked at them apologetically and announced that there would be no judgements or personal audiences with the king for the entire day once again.

'Another day in paradise,' Zimri sighed sarcastically under his breath. He fought to control the anger rising up in him and stomped hastily out of the throne room with Tibni following closely at his heels, their sandals slapping the shiny marble floor.

Right behind him Tibni whispered the question on both their minds, 'Do you think he even cares that the nation is at war and in dire peril?'

'All that pathetic fool cares about is his next golden goblet of wine!' snapped Zimri angrily, annoyed at being made to look like a fool in front of his men for the umpteenth time, he felt that king Elah was wasting his time when he had so many pressing issues to deal with, like securing Israel and plotting to rid the nation of the incompetent ruler and weakness it was wallowing in.

He was supposed to report to the throne room every morning as ordered by the king to receive any new information or developments necessary for his troops, he was to give Elah any feedback on the safety aspects of the city and of the possibility of any threats, but most days King Elah didn't even pretend to be interested by bothering to pitch for the report on the conditions and safety of *his* capital city. Leaving Zimri to do what he could without his king's input, not that he felt he needed any help from the idiot and his side-kick Chamberlain, but what enraged Zimri was that Elah had a duty to his subjects and he was neglecting it sorely.

'So...what's the plan?' inquired Tibni knowing beyond a doubt that the time was ripe for action, lowering his voice a fraction and leaning in closer to Zimri to avoid being overheard by any curious passers-by. They were walking together around the walls, checking the guard posts and making sure all the men had obeyed their orders and completed their duties properly during the previous shift.

Zimri believed in being visible when leading. He could not respect anyone who led from anywhere but the front lines. He set a fearsome example and made sure his men felt his presence and knew he was there with them in the thick of whatever situation. They also knew about his terrible temper and were careful not to provoke his rage, they identified the steak of sadistic pleasure he took in whipping them personally if they were brought to him on charges of insolence or incompetence, so the men went to great pains to ensure that there was never any cause whatsoever for corporal punishment to come their way from their commander.

Zimri quickly outlined his plan to Tibni; he kept his face expressionless and watched Tibni for any sign of deception. He knew he could slit Tibni's throat there and then at the slightest hint of betrayal and would feel nothing for doing it. He was not weighed down by a pesky conscience and had killed for far less before, but Tibni just stared at him in admiration, respecting his friend's courage and nerve. Zimri felt like he had just received an omen guaranteeing him success in his plan, that is, if he believed in that sort of nonsense.

'It's brilliant!' exclaimed Tibni and was quickly shushed by Zimri before they attracted any unwanted attention. The outburst had drawn a few curious stares from peasants in the street, but they soon turned back to their menial tasks and the two soldiers were once again ignored and continued their quiet discussion undisturbed. They were passing the city gates and Zimri stepped to the side to avoid a large pile of horse manure in the middle of the street. Tibni looked at the guard standing closest to him and signalled to him to get the mess cleaned up immediately. The two continued into the city along the streets that wound through the market place while they talked.

The market was loud with traders and merchants shouting their wares. There were brightly coloured linens from Egypt, beautifully woven carpets from as far away as Persia, black goat hair tents woven by the locals and a few pathetic looking slaves were standing dejectedly on an auction block to their left. The dust in the streets was making the air look like a golden haze shimmering in the heat. A bead of sweat ran down Tibni's back and he looked around at the mass of beggars sitting in the gutters calling out for food and any kind of mercy.

Zimri knew from his spy network that the king had arrived back at the palace shortly after dawn during the fourth watch and was carried straight to his bed-chamber by his eunuchs. He had stuck to his usual pattern of daily feasting and consuming massive amounts of fine wine at Arza's house and then being brought back to the palace unconscious by his trusted eunuchs. There would be no king until late that afternoon and then he would only get out of bed when it was time to leave the palace once more and go to repeat the cycle at his chamberlain's house.

'The king will probably not be seen at all today, he never summons us after the morning reports, but if anyone should be looking for me, make something up to cover for me…will you?' asked Zimri looking at Tibni, his cold eyes assessing his loyalty once again, after all, this wasn't a battlefield where they fought as a team and depended upon one another while they had each other's backs, this was high treason they were discussing and if Tibni double-crossed him to gain favour and went to the king, Zimri would be tortured and executed within the hour.

CHAPTER TWELVE

A few more days passed slowly and uneventfully with the daily routine never varying and a bored, relaxed mood fell over Zimri's troops in the city. The days were passed doing the same mundane duties and checks and then every afternoon at about the same time, Zimri handed over the leadership reins to Tibni for a few hours until just after sunset.

'Where have you been going every day?' asked a curious Tibni, one afternoon. He knew full well what Zimri was up to and what was going on but deciding to play the part of an innocent simpleton to cover his own back just in case, for some reason, Zimri's plan was discovered and he was caught. Tibni was not going to go down with his friend if it could be avoided.

Zimri winked at Tibni and said in an assuring tone: 'Don't worry too much, the less you know right now the better. Trust me on this, but meet me at the gates after sunset tonight.' Zimri instructed as he looked down at his friend, Tibni felt a cold shudder creep down his spine as he looked up at Zimri, a huge hulking figure filled with violence and malice.

Zimri had commanded his men not to leave their posts; he had them surrounding the palace and the city at strategic points along the wall, in the watch towers and at the gate. 'No one moves until I return.' He ordered as He left to carry out his plan.

It was early afternoon and the sun was warm on his face, he whistled a catchy tune as he strolled leisurely along the road once more. It was not long before he saw the house in the distance across the fields and left the road to take a shortcut. The ground was spongy and moist beneath his soft sandals, it was covered in thick luscious grass and densely growing bushes with flowers scenting the hot dry air with their sweet perfume. The crops in the field gave him cover from the house so he would not be noticed approaching the building from this direction by the slaves working there.

The house was white washed with a black slate roof and stood beautifully in the sunlight, the green grass and flowers around it contrasting brightly against the white walls. The heat made it appear to shimmer in the picturesque landscape and the songs of birds added to the beauty of the setting. There was a small stream flowing through the field in front of the house and as Zimri crossed over it, he stopped to drink deeply of the fresh, clean, cool water and splash some over his face. Once refreshed, he continued carefully on his way, crouching low as he neared the boundary of the property.

The wall around the garden was not very high, made of uncut rocks piled on top of each other and white washed to match the house, Zimri had no trouble launching himself over it when he was sure there was no one about. This was the first time he had gone over the wall, all his previous reconnoitring missions had been from under the bushes behind the wall, he had used it as cover to watch his prey, observe their habits and study their behaviour to give him any advantages necessary.

He hid himself under some big bushes in the garden and could see the road and the entrance to the house clearly from where he was. The slaves were preparing the evening meal, scurrying around finishing off their chores for the day before their master's arrival home; they would soon be dismissed for the night after his dinner and only return again in the early hours of the morning. The routine so far had never deviated; Arza was a creature of habit, obsessed with the tiniest detail, learning his routines had been almost too easy for Zimri.

He had watched the monotonous and predictable activities at the house for a few days now studying his prey very intently, enjoying stalking around like the predator that he was. Everyone had been so absorbed in their menial tasks that it was a simple matter to slip quietly into the garden undetected. The only real discomfort was the sun beating down in the heat of the day and having to lie absolutely still for hours in the cramped position to avoid being seen by the servants. He could hear the gentle bubble of the stream flowing not far away and his thirst intensified thinking of the cool clear water nearby.

It still irked him, as he lay in the shade of the bushes thinking of how Omri and King Elah had cheated him. 'Only half the chariot force, what an insult! After all I have done! How could Omri be chosen over me?' He'd asked himself that question repeatedly since Omri's promotion and could still not come to any other conclusion but that they were dishonest and corrupt. He had proven his worth repeatedly in battle, had killed more of the enemy than any other chariot driver, or soldier ever, he never shrunk back in horror at the ferocious clashes he had taken part in, yet he was rewarded with only a small piece of the prize!

He deserved so much better than that and he was going to forcibly take what he deserved! A lizard ran over his leg startling him from his reverie, he heard the sound of horses and a carriage in the distance coming along the road, getting steadily closer, but from where he lay, he could not see it yet, he lay still, and waited...

The carriage eventually came into his limited view and his heart raced as he battled to control the urge to jump up there and then and slash the chamberlain to pieces, the desire was so strong, almost uncontrollable, he needed to make someone bleed but there were just too many witnesses about and potential risks involved and with an extreme effort his common sense took over, he continued to focus his mind on the task at hand and took deep even breaths to keep the longing for blood at bay.

Arza had arrived home from the palace just before sunset as usual. His carriage had drawn up and his servant helped him down the steps, the breeze had the scent of his expensive perfume floating lightly on it and he was fusing about needing to change his robes before dinner because the king was on his way. 'I hope you fools have not over-cooked the lamb again.' he whined in his child-like voice as he walked into the house through a door held open by a lovely young slave girl.

The aroma of roasted lamb was heavy on the breeze and Zimri realised with a sharp pang that he was very hungry as his stomach grumbled and his mouth watered at the smell of the delicious food inside. It had cooled down a little by then, much to his relief and the lengthening shadows aided in his concealment. He was uncomfortable, thirsty and famished, his tunic was plastered against his back, he was sure that if someone sniffed the air, they would smell him there, all sticky and drenched in sweat.

CHAPTER THIRTEEN

Shortly after Arza arrived home, the sun hung just above the horizon like a heavy jewel from a chain, and in the twilight gloom, Elah, the king of Israel, arrived in his litter. The twelve heavily muscled eunuchs surrounding the litter were also the king's personal bodyguards; they were huge mountains of men, their muscles bunched and bulked under their tightly fitted short tunics, their bare feet making no sound on the well-worn smooth dusty road, the hair on their heads was shaved off, they were completely bald, a sign of shame or disgrace among the Israelites.

They were highly skilled fighters, personally trained and hand-picked by Ahab, Omri's son, who was reputed to be one of the best warriors in the entire kingdom, with the use of the sword, spear and the bow; he could shoot arrows further than any of the other men in his chariot force. The twelve men carried the heavy litter effortlessly between them as though it did not contain the overweight bulk of the alcoholic king and placed it at the gate gently, they stood back smartly at attention waiting for the king to appear.

One of the eunuchs, the captain - Zimri had never bothered to learn their names because he saw them as less than men - opened the side curtain and the king stood up with great difficulty from his elaborately cushioned chair. His richly coloured purple and gold embroidered robes fluttered delicately on the cool evening breeze, held in place on his shoulder by a large weighty golden pin that was moulded expertly to look like a rose encrusted with gem stones on the beautifully ornate petals and leaves.

Elah climbed out of the litter clumsily aided by the biggest of the eunuchs, the king took the proffered hand to help him ease his considerable bulk out of the litter's side as his obese body struggled to move unaided. The eunuchs stood silently, their eyes scanning the surrounding area and Zimri held his breath as one of them seemed to be looking directly at him, but after a moment that felt like an eternity to Zimri, the twelve lined up smartly around the king as he stood outside his litter regaining his composure and straightening his robes.

Elah enjoyed the trappings of luxury very much and his wide waistline straining against the beautiful red sash tied as a belt was a testament to his love of food and wine. He wore only purple dyed Egyptian cotton or silk robes traded in Egypt that came from some unknown land far away and to the East.

The colours purple, red and blue were extremely expensive and very rare, usually only worn by royalty, the dye was imported from Phoenicia, extracted a drop at a time from the Murex shellfish found in the waters of the Mediterranean Sea. King Elah took it to excess, like he did the wine and fine foods, having a new purple robe specially made and imported for his increasingly growing fat body every few days.

The crown on his head over his shoulder length limp, greasy black hair caught the final rays of the setting sun, and the jewels sparkled and winked at Zimri, he stared transfixed back at the twinkling rubies and marvelled in the fact that they looked just like perfect droplets of blood, just like on his dagger... He took it for another sign ensuring his success. The king walked slowly and awkwardly, struggling with his overweight figure, surrounded completely by his guards to the front door of Arza's house.

A guard knocked and opened the door before the king had reached the threshold so that his royal package would not have to stand outside like a commoner waiting for admittance. Elah stepped over the threshold heavily and disappeared into the house greeting Arza warmly. Once the king was safely inside, his voice could be heard from where Zimri lay dismissing his stony-faced mountainous eunuchs until the following morning. The king would soon be alone in the home of his chamberlain, just like most nights…

Behind the house were the slave's quarters, and the kings guards headed straight for the buildings there. They were all in a relaxed mood, just another normal day like any other, and they enjoyed not having to carry the king's increasing weight around for a short while.

Before long, the sounds of revelry could be heard as the lower class partied the night away, with plenty of wine and loud joking accompanied with loud laughter; the eunuchs had long-before befriended the staff at the house out of necessity due to their long hours spent there and enjoyed eating and drinking together with them as they relaxed after their heavy load was deposited.

One of the eunuchs began singing a song, his clear crisp voice like that of a young boy was lovely to listen to and the sound carried to where Zimri lay hidden. He smiled a cold vicious smile, because he knew they would not hear anything above the noise they were making and would be of no obstruction to his plan.

An owl hooted in the distance and the insects were adding their chorus to the symphony of night music. Something was scratching in the dirt near to Zimri, 'A field mouse or rat perhaps.' he thought absently. His senses were heightened, the scent of the freshly turned earth around where he lay was intoxicating, he could smell the expensive perfume the king and Arza were wearing wafting through the open window on the evening breeze, he saw the candles flicker slightly as the cool air moved through the main room disturbing the air where his prey sat as he waited, he itched to strike, the compulsion almost beyond his control, almost more than he could bear.

The evening meal was cleared away by the remaining servants and the last of the slaves were dismissed for the night. 'We won't need you again tonight, Mark.' said Arza as the slave placed another pitcher full of wine on the table. The slave bowed low to the king and exited the room hurriedly to join his friends in the slave's quarters at the back of the property.

'More wine, my king?' Arza's high-pitched voice carried out to where Zimri lay and he heard the wine splash into the golden goblets as it was poured.

'Can ducks float?' replied the king and burst into a fit of giggles at his own witticism.

'My lord is so hilarious.' Arza chuckled in a sugary tone. 'I saw a messenger arrive from General Omri today, was he bringing any good news on the siege?'

Zimri's ears pricked up at that question, there had been a few suggestions in his force that there was a spy close to the king, and that it was the reason Israel was raided so often by the Philistines. Up until that moment Zimri had dismissed the rumours as idle gossip, and his own spy network had been unable to come up with any concrete information or leads on any clandestine Philistine infiltrations. The fact that the king was too useless in Zimri's opinion and could not know or do anything of any value or importance had clouded Zimri's judgement and made him believe that there was no internal danger, but hearing Arza now, he was suddenly not so sure.

The entire siege was being handled by General Omri and fortunately, he did not need the idle king's help or advice with anything, so the spy could not have gotten any really vital information from Elah for the Philistines to use against Israel.

'Another justifiable reason.' he thought with righteous satisfaction. He was even more convinced that he was doing the right thing tonight, killing two birds with one stone; Arza was not going to be an innocent casualty, but another intended target!

'Yes, a few of the siege engines are in desperate need of repairs, blah…blah, and the soldiers need more supplies, food and weapons et cetera, you know the usual tiresome reports.' moaned the king slurring his words slightly, 'Omri says the inhabitants of Gibbethon are starving and shouldn't be able to hold out much longer, I don't understand all the complexities of what he does, he keeps the Philistines and the other bad guys in check, he makes me look good,' giggled Elah childishly. 'That's all I care about.' He hiccupped and held his goblet out to Arza for another refill.

'To the speedy surrender of Gibbethon and a resounding victory to Israel!' cried Arza drunkenly in his nasal voice as he lifted his goblet in a mock toast, sloshing wine all over himself.

'Don't waste good wine my friend!' chided Elah as he leaned back in his chair settling his massive bulk comfortably against the back of a loudly protesting chair.

The wine was doing its job, paralyzing the minds of the men so dependent upon it. Zimri waited for the opportune moment. The moment when the two men in the house had drunk too much and wouldn't be able to put up any kind of resistance, not that he thought they could ever be capable of escaping him, they were both weak, arrogant, good for nothing, cowards, but he didn't want them alerting the slaves or the guards at the back of the house because he was severely outnumbered and didn't relish the thought of taking on all the king's eunuchs at once.

Chapter Fourteen

Eventually after long hours of lying motionless, Zimri eased his cramped legs and smoothed his light tunic as he crawled out from under the bushes. He gently dusted any leaves or dirt from his clothing, and he strolled casually towards the front door; his soft leather sandals making no sound on the fancy brick pathway. To anyone watching, he gave all appearances of bringing an innocent message to the king, for the moment that was, so as not to raise the alarm prematurely.

He knocked on the door softly.

'Who could that be at this hour?' slurred Arza in irritation as he rose from his chair and stumbled awkwardly to the door.

'I did leave a message at the palace to find me here if any important business or communications came for my urgent attention.' sighed Elah. 'I apologize for the intrusion Arza, but a king's work is apparently never done.' He placed his elaborately decorated golden goblet on the table and turned towards the door as it swung open, he immediately recognized Zimri standing there and grimaced.

'This had better be important,' snapped Elah arrogantly, 'You should be at the palace protecting my wives and children.'

'My lord, it's vitally important...' snarled Zimri as his hand holding his dagger shot up with inhuman speed and slashed across Arza's throat. The blood splattered in Zimri's face making him look savagely demonic and he licked the blood from his lips slowly, savouring the salty, metallic taste and the king, in stunned disbelief, fell backwards off his chair paralyzed by shock, the crown rolled along the floor and came to rest in some ashes in front of the fire place.

Zimri saw the crown and thought to himself that it was rather symbolic, being in the ashes, 'from ashes to ashes-the end of a dynasty.' he said cheerfully and smiled wickedly as he stepped over Arza's lifeless corpse and took a few strides towards the panicking King Elah, who was crawling on the ground, grovelling, clawing at the floor in terror.

'Please, I will give you gold...command of...what do you want?' he cried out hysterically. 'It's yours...just please...please don't hurt Me.' he cried petrified. Elah looked up at Zimri's face and saw only death there, he cringed helplessly, realizing that there was no hope of survival tonight.

Zimri was enjoying the performance, intoxicated with the power he felt, drawing it out for as long as possible, he watched the king crawl and beg for his life, but the bloodlust was growing steadily once again and only the king's blood spilled would ease it now.

He bent down over the king and grabbed a handful of his greasy hair, lifting his head at a tilt to look down into his terrified eyes. He spat a large yellow glob of phlegm into the king's face, his spit running down the Elah's sagging cheeks and said with a soft confident voice: 'I want you dead.'

Panic consumed the king and his face paled even further at that last remark, his eyes were huge, wide, bulging orbs, his mouth opened and closed repeatedly as if he could not put into words a single thought and a dark patch had spread slowly down his expensive robes as his bladder released its contents and the stench of urine permeated the air.

Zimri toyed with his dagger along Elah's face, tickling him with it gently, teasing him with fear, prolonging the agonizing terror and delight in the supremacy he had over the most sovereign person in the kingdom. And then slowly, deliberately, he pushed the blade into the king's flabby neck, easing it in between the folds of skin gradually finding the main artery, a slow pain filled fraction of a millimetre at a time. The king was a pitifully paralysed lump of blubbering lard, he couldn't resist, he could only wait for the death that was creeping slowly closer to eventually carry him away.

Blood spurted over Zimri's hand making the knife handle slippery and sticky all at once. He wiggled the handle slightly to release the suction on the blade and pulled it out again very slowly. King Elah made a choking sound as his huge body collapsed under him; his blood spurted sporadically from the wound in his neck with each dwindling pulse.

Zimri pulled a chair closer and sat down on it casually and watched in fascination as the king hopelessly tried to stem the blood flow from the wound in his neck, writhing on the floor in an agonizingly futile attempt to live, painting patterns on the ground in his own blood until finally he laid still and his eyes stared straight ahead, unseeing and devoid of life.

Blood dribbled slowly down the blade of the dagger and splashed lazily onto the floor, time had paused...frozen at that moment, everything was forgotten except the hypnotic sadistic pleasure Zimri felt. Relishing in the sensation, he watched his masterpiece intently as the blood pool around his victims spread with a sluggish steadiness. Slowly, he looked up from the life-blood spilling onto the floor where the two bodies lay crumpled, and wiped his blade clean on the first victim's expensive purple robes. He spat on the ground deliberately next to the bodies, his spit mingling with the blood, a further insult to the dead, and he felt no remorse for his actions, just a man doing what needed to be done... a man taking out the garbage. He had come to Arza's house for this single purpose. He was not afraid to take what he wanted and he wanted the crown of Israel...

Zimri eventually roused himself from his blood fogged stupor and left the bodies in the house where they had fallen; the stench of blood, urine and excrement mingling together was terrible. He had cut the king's little finger off his flabby hand to remove the ring with the royal seal in it and had placed it on his own finger, he picked up the crown from the ashes on the floor, dusted it off and placed it carefully into a fold in his tunic.

He had not worn his armour tonight, so as to move quietly and comfortably and travel around unnoticed, just another peasant in the fields that no one ever paid any attention too. He went into the back of the house where the silent kitchen was and grabbed a large chunk of lamb, he took a bite into the delicious juicy meat and decided that the food was too good to pass up, he was starving so he sat down at the kitchen table contentedly and ate his fill of the roasted lamb cooked perfectly in garlic and herbs with delicious potatoes and onions and the softest bread.

The oily juices dribbled from his lips and into his close cropped pointy beard, it was the best meal he had eaten in a very long time and he poured himself a goblet of the fine wine to wash the food down with. He drank deeply to his success and toasted his own genius and cunning. The wine was delicious, not like the fermented sour vinegar they drank night after night in the brothel, but fruity and full of delightful refreshing delicate flavour. He rolled it around in his mouth appreciatively as he savoured all the flavours of the luxurious gourmet meal that he had just enjoyed.

Strolling nonchalantly out into the night, he smiled happily to himself, proud of his accomplishment, content knowing that leaving the dead bodies unattended too was a further insult to the king and his chamberlain, they should have been continuously attended to, washed in the proper way with candles burning permanently, until they were buried within twenty-four hours of their death.

He laughed softly to himself at the thought of what he had accomplished! He was the king now and he was heading straight to the palace to claim his well-earned prize.

CHAPTER FIFTEEN

Tibni, having his part to play in what Zimri was up to and doing exactly as he was told, was waiting nervously for Zimri, concealed in the shadows at the city gate, 'Is it done?' he asked in a conspirators whisper as he slithered out of the dark hiding spot to join his friend.

'Yes.' came the curt reply and he pulled the crown out from the fold in his tunic, Tibni gasped in astonishment, and bowed down before him.

'Did you talk to the men?' asked Zimri matter-of-factly, and was pleased when Tibni nodded his ascent, 'they are all behind you one hundred per cent and without any doubt.'

Not needing to be told what to do, having discussed the plan in detail before this moment, Tibni blew his horn sharply, just one short blast, and the chariot force under Zimri's command appeared in formation before them within minutes. They all stood rigidly, patiently waiting, eager for their next orders, looking at their new king with a healthy mix of fear and respect. Each man giving his oath to Zimri and awaiting their rewards that had been promised by Tibni for their loyalty to Zimri.

'I live, I fight, and if necessary, I will die for you my lord, King Zimri. Long live King Zimri!' cried Tibni with admiration and enthusiasm fuelling his high pitched voice.

The men all cheered together loudly, 'Long live King Zimri! Long live King Zimri!' They were stamping their feet and spear butts into the ground in unison and the noise was the sweetest sound Zimri had ever heard, the symbolic heartbeat of the new life of his kingdom.

'If only my father could see me now,' he thought to himself as he smiled proudly down at the warriors gathered before him. When the din had eventually quietened down a little, he turned to Tibni and embraced him like a brother.

They performed a makeshift vow ceremony, an ancient custom going back countless generations that was recited throughout the region to swear allegiance to a new king. For the benefit of the men standing before them, Zimri placed his large right hand on Tibni's scrawny left shoulder weightily, and asked with grave solemnity, 'Do you, Tibni, son of Ginath, solemnly swear to make my friends your friends and my enemies, your enemies?' Tibni, in return, placed his small right hand on Zimri's left shoulder, and in a sincere solemn tone, he replied: 'I do so solemnly swear.'

The oath was repeated throughout the men standing there, each one came forward individually to bow low and offer their loyalty, fealty and swords to Zimri personally. Each soldier pledging his allegiance on pain of death to the new king, and Zimri waited patiently, accepting each oath gladly, glorying in the commitments made to him, for each pledge bolstered his pride and self-esteem more.

Once all the men had given their oaths of fealty, Zimri looked around at his warriors, and signalled for silence, 'There is someone I would like to introduce to you!' He spoke with authority, playing his new role to perfection. 'The new general of the army of Israel-*my* army, is Tibni, son of Ginath!' He roared his friends name loudly and clapped Tibni on his back, nearly knocking the small man off his feet, and then shook Tibni's hand formally as the men cheered and roared their approval.

'Now we go into *my* palace, you are to be my royal guard and bodyguard; there will be rich rewards for those who serve me faithfully!' He turned towards the palace and shouted, 'Come!' he motioned for the men to follow him. 'To your new posts!' he said with a flourish waving his men through the entrance into the royal residence.

Once inside the palace, walking through the familiar corridors to the throne room, Zimri shouted at the top of his voice. 'The King Elah is dead!' His men followed at a quick march, disciplined and lethal. Their sandals were echoing along the corridors loudly as they stamped their feet in rhythmic unison, marching proudly with their hero, their commander and their king.

The cry was echoed by his soldiers, 'The King Elah is dead! King Zimri claims the throne of Israel!' His chariot force formed a tight ring around him, leading him to the throne room. He felt on top of the world, the crown balanced on his head, a conquering hero who had no one standing in his way.

The blood lust was beginning to dim down a little and he wanted to hold on to the high he was riding, to the emotional rush he had felt at the house of Arza.

He saw fear and disbelief etched on the faces of those servants who had stumbled from their beds. Tibni gave a quick signal and one of his men butted a servant who was standing in their way in the face with the back of his spear, which pleased Zimri, feeding on their alarm, seeing their horror gave him that sense of power he craved and could only have dreamed of before tonight.

'What happened?' asked a head strong and very beautiful chamber maid named Micah. She had only been working in the palace for a few months now and was one of the junior servants. Her mother and father both held high positions on the palace staff and were allowed to live in their own home outside of the palace complex. When Micah had turned seventeen and was still not betrothed to a man because of her independence and fiery strong will, her parents had brought her and her cousin Leah to work and live at the palace.

Zimri singled her out, his eyes flickering slowly over her tall lean body emphasised by the long fitted tunic she wore, he walked through the crowd now assembled to right in front of her. His face was a mask of wicked hunger, emanating evil and Micah stared defiantly back into his cold soul-less black eyes. He slapped her hard through the face, snapping her head sharply to the side, then he grabbed a handful of her long dark silky hair, twisting it around his hand and snapping her head back further so he could look menacingly down into her eyes and whisper breathily, 'I killed him...' her soft brown eyes grew wide and round with shock in her pretty face, he could not decide if it was defiance or fear he saw written there, he licked at the trickle of blood that had escaped from Micah's split lip and ran in a thin ribbon down her chin. The enjoyment was evident on his face and she shuddered involuntarily with revulsion as his tongue slithered down her chin licking up the copper tasting blood once more.

He savoured his brutal strength and her futile weakness, his control over her meaningless life, and then without loosening his grip on her hair, he dismissed the palace staff. A man jumped forward and asked for permission to speak, but one of the guards knocked him down with a backhanded slap to the face silencing him immediately. The man got up stiffly, his eye already beginning to swell and turning a dark blue, he turned to return to his bed with the rest of the staff, they hurried away like coach roaches scuttling away to some dark hiding place.

'You're hurting me,' whimpered a terrified Micah, a tear rolled from the edge of her eye towards her ear as Zimri roughly yanked her head up towards his face again, he licked the trail of the tear too, and she squirmed and shuddered in his grasp, the tears springing involuntarily to her eyes at his degrading gesture. He was breathing hard now, his stinking breath rasping in her ear, fully aroused by the naked fear he saw in her eyes, he spoke in a low dangerous tone, knowing it would frighten her even more, 'You're coming with me.' And he headed for the king's bedroom, not relinquishing his hold on her silky long hair, he dragged her awkwardly, helplessly along with him.

His men stepped back into the shadows, unseen, giving him privacy but protection all at the same time. He knew they were going to enjoy this as much as he would and that he could count on their discretion if and when the time came.

Her screams could be heard throughout the palace for the rest of the night. She cried helplessly aware of nothing but the unending pain she was experiencing, she begged and fought for her life, but it just incited Zimri's appetite for wickedness more. His evil sadistic desires knew no limits; he bit a huge chunk of her flesh out above her breast and chewed it slowly leaning over her motionless spread-eagled body, forcing her to watch as he literally devoured her. He savoured the disgust and agony on Micah's face, and thoroughly enjoyed hurting her in strange and different ways, she didn't stop trying to fight him off and he delighted in how pointless her pitiful attempts were.

Fully satisfied by the time he sent the bloody and beaten, bruised and broken Micah back to her room with one of his men, she was barely conscious and unable to walk, so she had been carried away roughly like a sack of wheat over the shoulder of Asher. Zimri fell asleep and slept better than he had ever slept before, in the king's bed, in the king's bedroom, in the king's palace.

Chapter Sixteen

'Murderer!' screamed Miriam. 'She was my baby!' she wept, 'How could you?' Zimri heard the far-away cries through the thick heavy fog of deep sleep but paid them no notice; he simply rolled over and lapsed back into sweet, dreamless, unconsciousness...

'As surely as the Lord lives, I curse him!' shrieked Miriam through her tears. 'He will burn in the fires of hell for all eternity! Everything he ever does will be doomed to end in flames!' she cried hysterically and wailed collapsing into a sodden sobbing heap on the polished cedar wood floor. 'He killed my baby!' sobbed Miriam inconsolably, 'She was so young and beautiful, such a good girl, she didn't deserve that, how could he do that to her?' she asked exasperated and dissolved into a fresh wave of tears. The pain was unbearable as her grief enveloped her and tears raced down her glistening cheeks leaving twin trails in their wake, falling to the floor in fat heavy drops that splashed as they landed.

'I know Miriam,' said Abrim sadly, nervously trying to quiet his wife, the guards were watching the two servants closely with amused interest, he knew they were just waiting for an excuse to strike them, to punish them for the loud outburst. He patted his wife's long dark hair comfortingly as he held her shuddering body close to his chest. 'What he did is unthinkable,' he murmured softly into her hair. 'He deserves to be punished by God. He murdered the king and Arza and our little baby girl.' His voice was strained with the anguish he felt, his emotions were raw and he fought back the tears threatening his eyes, knowing he had to be strong for his wife.

'We need to prepare her body,' announced a broken-hearted Miriam.

Abrim sighed and in his most soothing voice explained gently, 'Mary is with her, preparing her body, washing her, so don't worry, all the proper funeral rituals are being carefully observed. There are many candles burning and her body will not be left unattended at all until Micah rests in our family tomb this evening, I promise.' His own grief was overwhelming and he tightened his embrace around his wife as a fresh wave of sobs shook her body again. His ankle length tunic was completely soaked in the front from their continuous twin streams of salty tears and he had ripped it open down to his waist as a sign of extreme anguish when he had found Micah earlier that morning, dead in her bed.

'It's not supposed to be like this, Micah was supposed to be here to see that we rest in our tomb, no parent should ever out-live their child.' He moaned gently filled with compassion at his wife's agonized suffering. He tilted her face up lightly with his fingertips to look down into her soft watery eyes, holding her face in both his hands, he leaned down and gave her a light kiss on her tear-stained cheek, then leaning close to her, his lips brushing lightly against her ear, he whispered softly: 'I need to send word to General Omri at Gibbethon about the events of last night. He must know what has happened here so that he can act swiftly in retaliation to make Zimri pay for all the wrong he has done.' Miriam looked around her innocently, checking to see if the guards were paying any attention to them, but they were not interested in the grieving of the two servants and were ignoring them completely. Choosing rather to remain ignorant of the consequences of their leader's actions.

The two looked exactly like what they were, an innocent mother and father distraught by the sudden loss of their only child and giving each other a small measure of comfort and solace. Abrim continued to whisper softly. 'The messenger must leave as soon as possible this morning, and will need some food and drink for the journey, but I need a way to get him out of the palace without Zimri's men noticing. It should be done secretly and quickly before we lose our window of opportunity.' He pulled away from the consoling embrace slightly to look down into his wife's upturned face, 'Do you have any suggestions?' He asked knowing that if he kept his wife occupied with the task at hand, it would help to keep her mind off of the painful sorrow she felt at losing their beautiful daughter.

'I don't think they know about the servants entrance through the kitchen yet,' replied Miriam softly as they walked together towards the kitchen, the corridor was deserted as the guards weren't stationed that far away from the king yet, but the two spoke in hushed tones anyway. 'The men are new in the palace, they are used to riding on their chariots to war,' she continued, 'Not standing around here waiting for a reason to hit someone.' she added barely moving her lips. 'It will have to be one of the kitchen girls,' she said thoughtfully, 'otherwise anyone else will be missed in the palace, besides I can easily explain a missing kitchen girl with the plausible story that I sent her to the market for food or supplies if they even notice. Leah is probably the best option.'

'No!' gasped a shocked Abrim, 'Not Leah…No!' shaking his head from side to side adamantly, but Miriam shushed him and continued with her logical reasoning, overruling his objection.

'She is sensible and smart enough to be sent on errands, I send her all the time.' She pointed out obstinately 'and besides the guards will be far less suspicious of a missing young girl than a boy or a man. The guards are not likely to hunt down a young kitchen girl, if they should happen to discover that she is missing – looks can be deceiving.' She clarified in her no nonsense tone.

Abrim knew that his wife had made her decision and there would be no point arguing with her any further, he reluctantly agreed that Miriam's plan was probably the best solution to getting someone out of the palace unseen and their absence unnoticed since they had been ordered that no one could leave or enter the palace without King Zimri's permission. He was uncomfortable, however, because they were gambling another innocent life, the stakes were very high and life was precious to him. He felt so guilty at risking anyone else to bring them the deliverance they needed.

He was worried about Leah because the guards were vicious and cruel in carrying out their new king's brutal orders and a young girl like Leah would not stand a chance if caught, she would never survive their sadistic tendencies, he had just lost his only daughter, he couldn't risk his niece's life too, not another innocent young girl with her entire life ahead of her.

Miriam had been in charge of the kitchen staff for twelve years now, she had begun working there as a junior cook when Baasha was the king and had worked hard to get to where she was. She was well liked and respected by all who worked for her and with her. She was known for her integrity and tenacity and for getting the job done, no matter the obstacle. She was a small woman, in her early forties, but her tiny frame was deceptive, she was strong, courageous and the toughest person Abrim had ever met. Her dark hair was liberally streaked with grey and the creases on her once very lovely face were a testament to the life she had lived to the fullest. Her smiling eyes were soft and shone with an inner peace and contentment, and she laughed often, believing to always make the best of every situation. But not today, Miriam suddenly looked old and worn as if someone had bleached the colour out of her very existence and left behind a tired and dull shell of her former vibrant self.

CHAPTER SEVENTEEN

Abrim feared that the loss of their child would irreparably break his beloved wife. He realised with a stab of grief that Micah had been very much like her mother and it was what he had fallen in love with, the fiery independence and brilliance had been what had attracted him to her the most, instead of driving him away like all the other suitors Miriam's parents had tried to enter into marriage negotiations with.

The men in the Jewish community liked quiet and submissive wives who did what they were told when they were told and without question and they kept their mouths shut. A good wife did not voice her opinions about anything her husband said in their culture. Miriam had always been very open and outspoken and voiced her opinion regularly, which when coupled with her intelligence was not viewed as 'proper womanly behaviour' in their beliefs, but she had never disobeyed or disrespected her husband and Abrim thought that her submissiveness was even more substantial since she was so intelligent, choosing to obey him rather than mindlessly being forced to.

She never opposed a decision he made but would often quietly give him her thoughts on the matter when Abrim was faced with difficult decisions, she knew he valued her input and once he had weighed all his options, and his decision was made, she stood behind him whole-heartedly whether she agreed with him or not.

Abrim loved the depth of Miriam's loyalty to him and thanked God daily for giving him such a highly 'improper', unconventional, and intelligent wife. Her strong personality and will to face any

challenge head-on would have lived on in their daughter, except…
their daughter was dead…dead. Abrim's grief threatened to
overwhelm him again and he dashed a tear away angrily with the
back of his hand.

'If anyone would know what to do, it will be the General,'
Abrim said softly dragging his thoughts back to the task at hand,
'for now though, just do as you're ordered please and keep out of
Zimri's way if possible,' he pleaded with his wife, urgency filling
his voice and fear clouding his soft brown eyes. Taking her hands
in his, he kissed her fingertips lightly and told her that he could not
bear to lose her too, and that the guards were just waiting for any
excuse…

'Promise me you'll do the same,' was Miriam's whispered
response, 'My heart is broken so badly already, and poor sweet
Leah, I still have to tell her, she doesn't even know yet that she's
just lost her cousin and best friend.' A trace of a sad smile flitted
quickly across Miriam's lips as she thought of the close bond the
two girls had forged over the years. Pulling her drifting thoughts
back to the painful present, she added, 'She should be back from
the neighbouring village by now where I sent her yesterday to get
some fresh onions.' Miriam started to cry again and the tears ran
freely and unchecked down her face. 'I'm sending her out to who
knows what.' Her voice choked with hopelessness, and she blew her
nose noisily on a scrap of cloth. She stood up on her tiptoes to give
her husband a gentle kiss on the cheek and said tenderly: 'I won't be
able to get out of the kitchen again until we're dismissed later this
evening; I don't want to draw any attention to Leah being missing,
so I'll have to do all her work for the day too.'

'Alright, my love.' answered Abrim. 'Micah would want us to
be strong for each other, if we can give her nothing else, let's give
her that, and I'll see you later to lay our daughter to rest,' he said,
embracing his wife lovingly one more time and trying to offer what
little comfort he could. Miriam nodded her head against his chest.
Tearing herself away, she looked up into his face and gave him a sad
but determined smile, 'God's will be done.' She said bravely as she
walked determinedly into the kitchen.

The day passed agonizingly slowly for Abrim, he had no way of knowing if their plan had been successful or not. Did Leah get caught or did she forget the message? Girls could be so unreliable and flighty sometimes, perhaps she got out of the kitchen and then panicked and decided to go to the guards or refused to go altogether. His paranoia was driving him insane and the waiting was the worst torture he could imagine, time was dragging by so slowly, it was still at least two more hours before he could take his wife and daughter to their family tomb.

He tried to keep himself busy to settle his nerves and he was sure that the guards were suspicious of his every move; a little while earlier he was positive that he was being followed. 'Steady now Abrim,' he chided himself quietly, 'act normally, you could blow the whole thing just by being over paranoid,' and he continued carefully with his normal responsibilities around the palace complex.

All the servants were coming to him throughout the afternoon to find out if any of their chores or obligations were to change in anyway but Abrim reassured them all that until they were commanded by the king – their duties would remain exactly the same.

There were horrible rumours that the men who rode in Zimri's chariot unit could keep a man alive in the worst possible, most excruciating pain during torture for at least five days while extracting information from him. An involuntary shudder ran down Abrim's spine as he thought about what he had heard and after seeing Micah's ruined and broken body this morning, he was not so sure that they were just stories at all.

Zimri had not emerged from the king's bedroom that day and the entire palace staff secretly hoped that he never would. Everyone who had worked in the palace before today was nervous and the tension could be felt, it was heavy in the air, and the fear was contagious, spreading through the staff faster than a bush fire through dry grass and no one wanted to get in the way of the guards or be Zimri's next victim.

Time stood still for Miriam too, after she gently broke the news to Leah, who cried and wailed loudly in the kitchen. 'Hush! Now child!' hissed Miriam sternly shocking Leah back to the dangerous situation they were faced with. 'We do not want the guards coming into the kitchen to see what all the fuss is about.' she murmured urgently against Leah's ear, her face pressed against Leah's cheek, and at the same time, squeezed her niece's hands reassuringly. 'Micah needs us to be strong and do whatever we can to avenge her and put a stop to this madman!'

Nodding silently, Leah asked: 'What can I do Aunt Miriam?' tears were flowing down her face in two steady streams over her cheeks.

'I need you to leave the palace through the servant's entrance,' she indicated the low door at the side of the kitchen that they had hardly ever used. It was half-hidden behind some sacks of grain and it led out to the courtyard where the watch guards slept when they were off duty. 'And somehow you must get to Gibbethon.' explained Miriam with a seriousness that forced Leah's practical brain began thinking of a sensible and logical solution.

'I will go now,' nodded Leah, 'Zach has horses; I think he will let me borrow one and maybe he even knows the way to Gibbethon too.' She was concentrating on the challenge ahead and thought through all the possible dangers like getting caught by the guards or bandits on the road. She knew her aunt would not have asked her if there was any alternative, so she resolutely lifted her chin and searched her heart for the courage she knew she needed. She hugged Miriam tightly and asked her aunt to pray for the success of her mission, her safety and guidance.

'Go with God.' said Miriam lovingly as she let her niece out of the small servants entrance, the small wooden door creaked and groaned with disuse and then she locked the loudly protesting door securely behind her, pulling a few of the heavy sacks of corn back to in front of the door to make it look like it had not been disturbed just in case the guards did come into the kitchen.

She ordered the other two kitchen girls to say that there had always just been the two of them and Miriam in the kitchens should the guards question them. The two girls, Anna and Sarah were sisters and loved Miriam very much, they solemnly promised before God that they would not mention Leah to anyone and Miriam trusted them, they were hard working and had been working in the kitchen with Miriam for a few years, they had never let her down before.

'Now then, let's begin to prepare our new king's dinner.' announced Miriam in her most business-like manner as she busied herself around the kitchen as though nothing had ever happened.

Chapter Eighteen

Leah checked behind her nervously as she made her way over to the stables where Zach worked with his father. She was terrified that she was being followed and zigzagged her way around the market place in an attempt to confuse anyone who might be watching her.

Zach was busy putting fresh straw into one of the stalls for his favourite mare. She was the oldest, softest natured horse in the stables but as sure footed and nimble as a young gazelle and didn't frighten too easily. Her rusty coloured coat with the black mane shot through with grey, reminded Leah of autumn leaves fallen on the fresh wet ground. His father had implied that the mare was getting too old and would soon have to be put out to pasture. Zach was miserable at the thought of his lovely horse just waiting to die out in the pastures. 'Sorry son, but she's of no use to the army anymore and doesn't bring us any coin.' His father had explained when Zach had confronted him. 'She can't breed now and she's not fast enough for the chariots, it costs a lot of money to feed and house her, and we just can't afford it!'

'Zach!' Leah hissed loudly trying not to alert anyone else to her arrival.

'Hey! What are you doing here?' he blurted out startled by her sudden appearance. 'Shouldn't you be in the palace cooking or something?' he asked, his brow furrowed deeply and his eyes were sad. Leah knew something was bothering her young friend.

'I need to get to Gibbethon,' she said in a conspiring whisper. 'Can I borrow one of the horses?'

'Whoa! Are you mad? You know my father will never allow that!' Leah just stood there silently with a beaten look on her face. 'Does he even have to know?' she asked quietly looking around her fearfully.

'Does this have anything to do with the weird rumours racing around the city about last night?' he asked in a curious soft voice. She hesitated at the question and Zach immediately knew that he had hit the nail on the head and wanted to help his friend. Seeing a solution to both of their problems, he looked around him carefully before answering: 'Alright, but I can only let you have this one,' he indicated his rusty coloured mare with a slight nod of his head, 'the rest of the horses are all here for the charioteers to use, and we don't want to alert them to a missing horse, which would make them ask some really serious questions.' he said while patting his old mare lovingly, 'She is a bit old but strong and reliable. She'll get you there safely enough and she won't be missed in the stable for a while,' his friendly face was smiling as he spoke but then he turned suddenly to Leah and her heart almost broke, she wanted to tell her young friend everything, and for an instant, she almost did, but then she looked away quickly from Zach's open and honest gaze and knew that she couldn't endanger him as well.

Zach looked at two soldiers marching past the stables and noticed Leah flinch slightly. He softly asked: 'What is going on?' He got no response from Leah and instantly guessed that the situation was urgent. He knew and trusted Leah and sprang into immediate action already putting the saddle on the mare while she fastened the leather straps and checked the reigns desperately trying to fill the awkward silence that had enveloped them.

'I can't tell you more then I already have,' Leah admitted sadly, 'I might have already put you and your dad in very real danger just by coming here - please don't tell anyone that you have seen me, and if anyone should ask about the missing horse, just say that I stole her.' she said in a low voice as she jumped up into the saddle and rode away at a calm gentle trot that belied the urgency she felt. She thought she would keep her pace casual so as to not attract any unnecessary attention, but once out of the city and away from any curious eyes, she pushed the mare to a faster gallop along the road heading to Philistia.

Zach had been true to his word, the mare was full of heart, she didn't seem to tire easily and once Leah was a few kilometres away from the outskirts of Tirzah, she decided not to push the horse too hard for too long so she slowed the pace to a more comfortable walk and kept the journey at a steady pace, once she was satisfied that she had put enough distance between herself and the horrors of Tirzah.

She was terrified, she had never been this far from home before, only venturing out to the farmlands just outside of the city a few times to help in the harvesting and going to the neighbouring villages around Tirzah for kitchen supplies and farm produce.

Zach had said that this road would lead her straight to the Israelite army and she started to panic as the sun began to set and it got steadily darker. She knew she would have to find a safe place to rest for both her and the horse away from the road, it was too dangerous to continue in the dark, the mare could stumble in a ditch and break a leg and then what would she do?

She moved off the road as the sun disappeared and found a cosy spot between some trees growing closely together and some think brush, it would serve as a natural barrier around the horse and herself. She tied the horse's reigns to a low tree stump, giving the mare enough room to graze and laid down in her cloak to get some rest but, sleep was not forthcoming.

Every time she closed her eyes; she imagined Zimri's leering face as he inflicted the terrible injuries to her cousin that her Aunt had described. She had no food with her and nothing to drink and she didn't want to wander around in the dark, also she was so afraid of being noticed by soldiers out on patrol, she wasn't sure how far the patrols around Tirzah travelled, or if they even did patrol at night, so she huddled down in her cloak and silently listened to the noises in the dark, alert and watching, able to make out the shapes of the trees, and harmless shrubbery around her by the silvery light of the bright full moon.

There were many predators outside of the city walls and Leah feared for herself and the old mare. Bandits roamed the countryside and were becoming more numerous now that Israel had fallen into decay over the last two years. Poverty and starvation drove many to desperation outside of the law. With the bulk of the army being away in Philistia, there was no one to keep the peace or law and order in the capital and to bring justice to the criminals, the countryside had become a death-trap to any traveller.

There was also the added constant danger of wild animals, bears, wolves and even lions roamed in search of prey and Leah was terrified at the prospect of all the potential dangers she faced in the dark. A fire was tempting to keep the wild animals at bay and would provide her with a little warmth in the cold night air, but she was afraid that it would attract the bandits or soldiers, so she opted for the cold dark silence to hide in and hoped she would not be discovered.

She lay still and alert like that all night long and thought to herself about the events of the past two days, she wandered how far she still had to travel and prayed to God for protection and the success of her mission. She and her family still worshipped the God of Abraham, Isaac and Jacob; they never practiced the idolatrous religion of the Golden Calf or any of the other strange new gods that were appearing in Israel lately. Leah believed that God had changed Jacob's name to Israel and then Israel had had twelve sons who had eventually become known as the twelve tribes of Israel, it was then only rational to worship the God of Israel in her opinion.

CHAPTER NINETEEN

'At last!' exclaimed Abrim with relief, they were finally dismissed by Tibni for the night. The day had passed without any further injuries or deaths, Miriam and Abrim paid the man who had brought the cart to the side entrance of the palace where Micah's body was waiting, she had been carefully washed and wrapped in pure white linen and Abrim gingerly lifted her body and gently laid her respectfully on the flower covered bed of the cart to be transported to their tomb.

Mother and father walked slowly with their heads bowed behind the cart with the body of their daughter on the back of it. Covered in a white linen shroud, surrounded by hyssop and anointed with myrrh, the body looked so small and vulnerable. The wailing was terrible to hear, so many of Micah's friends and family had come to mourn her passing, they were dressed in sack cloth and were covered in ashes. Abrim had shaved off his long beard in an outward display of mourning and anguish.

Micah had been loved by all who knew her and her death was a terrible blow and shock to everyone. Leah's absence from the funeral was immediately noticed and many of their family and friends inquired as to her whereabouts, knowing that the two girls had been more like sisters then cousins, inseparable with a bond so strong between the two girls, it was no surprise to Miriam that Leah would risk her life to avenge her cousin's vicious and senseless murder.

Abrim and Miriam had taken Leah into their home and raised her as their own when the girls were both ten years old.

Leah's parents had died during a violent raid on their village by Philistines; the young girl had barely escaped by hiding inside a basket of wheat at the threshing floor, a place that was fortunately overlooked by the violent attackers.

Abrim had mourned the loss of his younger brother deeply and had taken the orphaned Leah in immediately as was his duty according to the Law of Moses. Leah had quickly crept into their hearts and they into hers, at times Abrim and Miriam had to remind themselves that Leah was their niece, she felt so much like a daughter to them, and Micah had loved Leah like a sister. Miriam explained Leah's absence with the excuse that she was sick and unable to attend the funeral in case she made the entire proceedings or burial ritually unclean.

The procession made its way up to the tomb slowly and Micah was laid to rest with her father's family in the family burial chamber, a small cave with a large stone rolled over the entrance. It took several strong men to roll the stone away, and once inside, there was a shelf visible at the back of the tomb containing large ceramic jars filled with the bones of Abrim's long dead relatives. In the centre of the cave was a large solid table-like rock, hewn out of the mountain itself, it was smooth and rectangular in shape and seemed to be waiting patiently for the latest body to be laid upon it. Abrim and Miriam gently lifted their daughter's body and laid her onto the stone slab, they placed the large jar that would eventually hold Micah's bones at her feet. Only much later would the decorated jar join the other relatives on the shelf at the back of the tomb.

The air was musty and stale inside the small cave and the oppressive and heavy air atmosphere, scented with the fresh myrrh and hyssop that seemed at odds with the decay in the cave, was an outward reflection of their heavy hearts. Miriam wailed loudly and cried huge heavy tears, they fell in fat drops onto the unmoving form covered in the white shroud. Abrim prayed and the family and friends all said their final farewells to their beloved Micah. They then re-sealed the tomb again just as the sun slipped below the horizon and they all walked away slowly with their heads hanging disconsolately back to their homes in the twilight gloom.

Once safely back inside their own home, Abrim whispered softly to his wife, 'I think I was followed today, so keep your voice down. Did Leah get away as planned?' he asked softly.

'Yes, she slipped out, no one besides you, me and Leah know of her mission or that she is even missing,' replied his wife confidently, 'Anna and Sarah have promised before God not to mention that we are missing a kitchen girl, they don't know why Leah left or where she was going, just that all our lives depend on the guards thinking that it was always just myself and the two sisters in the kitchen.' explained Miriam breathily.

'Do you know if she is up for the task?' questioned Abrim sceptically, 'I mean…how she will get to get there? Gibbethon is thirty-five kilometres away, a day's travel on horse-back and only if you push the horse and if you know how to ride and know the treacherous roads. There are a hundred things that could happen to her between here and Gibbethon.' Abrim doubtfully expressed his concerns while he helped Miriam to prepare their meagre evening meal.

'We didn't exactly have our choice of the best messenger, Abrim,' snapped Miriam impatiently, 'But I'm confident that Leah is up for the task. I trust her. She left shortly after we spoke early this morning, and I know she can ride very well,' Miriam's tone softened as she continued to clarify, 'She said that she would not go to anyone, but that she would take the message herself in case of any spies in the city reporting back to Zimri and putting us all at risk of torture and death. I know the girl will do her very best, that's all we can ask of her. The rest is up to God.'

Abrim squeezed his wife's hand in a silent apology and added: 'She's a good girl, Micah would be so proud of her cousin.' And then he added thoughtfully: 'God doesn't always call the qualified, He qualifies the called…'

'She is very brave,' agreed Miriam. 'There is a boy she knows, a little younger than her, Zach, I think she said his name is,' Miriam continued softly, 'anyway he has horses and the stables his father owns are the ones the charioteers use to house their horses in, and since they are all so absorbed here in Tirzah with their new king and his atrocities, they have no need of their horses right now, besides she trusts him, so whether she went alone, or they went together, I do not know, but I am sure that Leah will get the message to General Omri somehow, she is extremely resourceful.' added Miriam still a little irked by her husband's lack of faith in Leah.

Abrim said goodnight to his wife, kissed her gently on the forehead and they retired for the night. 'Tomorrow will be another very hard day and we need to be strong and ready for it,' said Miriam. 'I love you. Sleep well.'

'I love you more then you know,' was the reply from Abrim. And surprisingly they both fell into an exhausted sleep and slept in each other's arms, giving comfort and warmth to one other.

CHAPTER TWENTY

Early the next morning Zimri ordered his men to round up all of the relatives of Elah and bring them to his throne room. 'Don't just bring me the puppies he sired, or the sows he called his wives and concubines!' he yelled 'I want *all* of the members – even distant relations - of the house of Baasha brought to me at once!' He was pacing back and forth in the throne room impatiently, dressed in purple royal robes, he looked every bit like the king he wanted to be. Proud and arrogant. Feared and revered.

The crown felt heavy on his head, but it was a wonderfully reassuring weight, like a heavy reminder of how far he had come. His jewelled sword swung regally from his leather belt as he walked proudly across the room and the dagger in his belt-razor sharp, gave him real comfort, he was never without it. He would always keep it close, he always had, it was his good luck charm.

He climbed the steps to the throne, sat down with a perfect and regal posture and hoped he looked magnificently fearsome and noble as he waited impatiently strumming his fingers on the arm of the throne, while one by one, every member of the family of Elah and his father Baasha and all their friends were all rounded up like sheep in a pen in front of him.

He smiled a cold reptilian smile as they stared up at him on the throne. He was caught up in the gratification of being the king; there was no one to tell him what to do or how to do it, he was all powerful. His men were lined up against the walls of the throne room; they knew what had to be done and were eager to get started.

It was customary for a new king to kill all surviving members of the previous dynasty to eliminate all opposing claimants to the throne. Zimri was just luxuriating in the moment of sadistic anticipation he felt before giving the final order and the families of the drunken, pathetic Elah and unfortunately, the great Baasha, would be put to death, wiping the dynasty from the face of the earth and placing them only in the history scrolls.

His men all looked up at him expectantly, they knew he liked the dramatic theatrics and enjoyed prolonging the suspense, the royal family knew it too. Each one of them knew why they were there, that they were all going to die, and then he gave the signal... Zimri stood and spread his hands. The guards all stepped forward in unison and grabbed a victim each; they were marched forcibly out of the throne room down to the parade ground below, which was directly under the throne room balcony. Zimri went over to the balcony as the doomed members of the dead monarch and his men made their way outside.

He stood in the fresh breeze, his purple robes flapped lightly around his ankles and he lifted his face to the sun feeling the warmth on his skin like a lovers caress. He looked down at the parade ground below and waited for the blood sport to begin. His heart was beating quickly with anticipation, he had never seen the deaths of so many people all at once before and the idea excited him, there would be so much blood, it was so exhilarating and then they appeared on the parade ground below him.

Zimri was slightly disappointed that he would not be shedding the blood himself, but he settled into his new role as king and decided to see if observing this many deaths at once would have the same satisfying effect as killing one person at a time with his own hand would have.

He figured the experiment would not hurt and if his lusts were not sated, he could find another victim easily enough in Tirzah to satisfy his cravings. He took deep even breaths to control his immediate desire, he needed to see the blood now, but this time he wouldn't be the one spilling it, so he had to get his satisfaction from watching from above, like a god. He certainly felt like a god, invincible and terrifyingly dominant.

Some of the women and children were crying, begging, pleading for their pathetic lives, others were trying to hold on to what little dignity they could and remained stony faced and quiet.

Zimri studied the scene before him in eager expectation and he watched as the men, women and children of all ages were slaughtered like sheep by the guards. Some were stabbed in their chests, some had their throats cut and died mercifully quickly, while some of them were hacked at as they had tried to run, receiving a few bloody blows that sliced into them before finally, they were cut down like wheat at harvest time to bleed dark pools out onto the ground. Zimri watched captivated by the violence below him and enjoyed the scene immensely.

There was blood everywhere, it spattered on the floor in pretty patterns or pooled in dark crimson shapes around the bodies as it leaked from the lifeless forms. To Zimri, the sight before him was beautiful, artistic, his masterpiece, his gift to the world. And he stood there for what felt like ages watching the sunlight reflect off the blood until it seeped into the ground leaving only dark muddy patches.

The guards had left the bodies undisturbed and unattended to as he had ordered and the silence of death was serene and peaceful and Zimri bathed in it.

A few stray dogs had been drawn to the parade ground by the coppery scent of the blood and excrement and had begun gnawing on the bodies, growling and snarling at one another as they chewed on limbs and fought over the bones. Carrion birds circled overhead and swooped down intermittently stripping the flesh quickly between the feeding frenzy of the dogs and then quickly flapping up loudly into the sky again to await the next opportunity to steal some of the fresh bloody meat.

The bodies were left like that to be devoured by the dogs and birds until after Zimri had finished his late dinner, long after sunset, just before dawn the next morning, he gave the order that what was left of the bodies was to be piled outside the city gates as a grisly warning to anyone who might want to challenge his power and authority and claim to the throne.

In that way he fulfilled what God said about Baasha's line, that it would not last because he killed Nadab, the son of Jeroboam, the very first king of Israel.

CHAPTER TWENTY-ONE

Outside the walls of Gibbethon,
A Philistine City under siege.

Omri woke up early, like he did every morning, he called for Dan, his young attendant, to bring him some clean water to wash his face with. Dan immediately ran to do his bidding, he fetched water from the nearby stream and then began heating it over an open fire so that his master would not have to wash in cold water.

Omri dressed quickly and sat brooding, as usual behind his table, he poured over his maps for hours on end. Staring at the surrounding regions as though the way into Gibbethon would jump up at him suddenly.

Dan looked over at his master and smiling, he quietly asked: 'Must I bring you some breakfast, sir?'

Omri looked up from his parchments and maps and smiled, 'It depends on what we're having today, because yesterday's bread looked a little suspect.' he replied winking at the young boy.

'I found some goat's milk and flat bread with cheese.' answered Dan eagerly.

'Good man!' exclaimed Omri, 'I am starving! Make sure you bring enough for the both of us, you need to put some meat on those bones if we're to make a warrior out of you.'

Dan scampered away to secure their morning meal and Omri's stomach protested loudly at being so neglected for so long.

The four months waiting outside the walls of Gibbethon were immensely frustrating for Omri who wanted to bring the siege to a quick and decisive end, hobbling the arrogant Philistines, if not totally annihilating them for being such a continuous burden to Israel. The inactivity and boredom was extremely dangerous to the army because they could easily fall into the slump and themselves become a target, if they were too used to the boring mundane tasks and let their guard down even a little, they would be vulnerable to attack.

Omri kept a strict regimen of discipline and weapons training for his men and regularly sent out scouting parties to harass the surrounding villages and farms, the men were placated by the sport and any talk of mutiny was immediately abandoned.

Ahab always led the scouting parties and often came back with captives who were desperately trying to escape the starvation and lawlessness inside the besieged city. The lack of food inside Gibbethon was not the only problem the citizens faced, dead bodies lay wherever they had fallen, forgotten and ignored in the daily struggle to survive. Funeral rituals and burials had long since been abandoned as no one had the strength or tenacity to keep up with the ever increasing piles of corpses. Disease spread rapidly through the streets of the city and thousands of its inhabitants succumbed to the death that silently stalked them.

Prisoners were always questioned very carefully and then were given a quick clean death. Omri hated the senseless killing, but did not have the resources available to keep the prisoners housed and fed at the camp. 'A dead enemy can't kill you tomorrow,' he explained to Ahab one day while the necessary executions were taking place. There was also the added danger that the Philistine captives were undercover soldiers sent out to be deliberately apprehended and to infiltrate the Israelite's camp in a desperate attempt to liberate their city, being able to attack the Israelites from inside their camp. Omri also couldn't afford to have any Philistines escaping and rallying reinforcements from any allied nations in the surrounding kingdoms.

CHAPTER TWENTY-TWO

'Father! I think you need to hear this!' called Ahab loudly, 'I have a very strange messenger from the palace!' The officer, Jared, standing guarding Omri's tent stood perfectly still but greeted his friend Ahab while he waited for permission to continue speaking at the entrance to his father's command tent.

Ahab had stopped Leah along the road leading into Philistia and the Israelite army camp while he was leading a scouting party in the nearby hills, and after hearing that she had ridden from Tirzah alone; he had decided that she should be taken straight to the general to deliver her message to Omri herself.

It was unheard of in their custom for a woman to travel alone; Ahab was convinced that the reason for the girl's arrival had to be serious enough to cause her to risk her life and reputation to reach them. She had almost fallen off her horse in exhaustion when he had stopped her and the men could see straightaway that both the animal and the girl were terrified.

Ahab had ordered his men to continue checking the area for any signs of new enemy activity during the previous night and had sent her windblown horse with one of his warriors straight to the stables to be cared for immediately. He had then escorted Leah directly into the camp directly to the general's tent.

It was very early, the smell of wood smoke from the morning cooking fires scented the air as the soldiers prepared to break their fast, the sound of muted conversations could be heard from around the camp as the army stirred and readied for another day of waiting for the Philistines to surrender to the army outside the walls of Gibbethon.

The tents were arranged neatly in straight rows and the colourful banners snapped on the crisp morning breeze, birds sang sweetly and the sky was clear and blue without the slightest wisp of cloud overhead. A bead of sweat ran from her temple down the side of Leah's face as she waited anxiously sandwiched between Ahab and Jared for the general to appear so that she could give him the horrible message she carried.

'What is it now?' grumbled a low voice from inside the black goat hair tent. 'Has King Elah fallen out of bed again or bumped his fat little toe?' enquired Omri in a sarcastic patronising tone as he stooped to exit through the low entrance. Immediately he knew something was terribly wrong when he spotted the girl standing awkwardly in the camp between his son and his trusted friend Jared.

She was dirty, dishevelled and visibly shaken, but he saw a resilient spirit in her eyes as he slowly looked her over. The dust was caked to her skin and her normally big brown, intelligent eyes were blood-shot and weary. Her robes were travel stained and Omri knew instantly that she had ridden to the camp in a dreadful haste. He tilted his head slightly and looked inquiringly at his son for the explanation about the morning's unlikely visitor.

'Father, this young woman was stopped along the road leading into the camp and she says she must speak with you only!' announced Ahab crisply, 'I brought her here when she said that it was urgent and secret and that she was sent by Abrim from the palace in Tirzah! She says that you know Abrim well and that she can prove that she's not a Philistine spy,' continued Ahab in a clear and confident tone.

Omri evaluated the situation in silence for what felt like ages to Leah as the young men nervously tried to ignore the serious breach in protocol, he knew his son and was proud of the man he was becoming. Ahab showed all of the strengths and skills that Omri admired and he was certain that his son would make a fine leader someday. Jared was a dependable young man and he had been watching him very closely for some time, Jared showed a lot of promise and potential on and off of the battle field. He was one of the warriors that Omri had a future plan for, and was being groomed for an upcoming leadership position in the army because he was quick witted and intelligent and Omri trusted in his discretion, loyalty and reliability.

'Go ahead, out with it!' snapped Omri impatiently, 'I don't have all day! I have a siege to finish.' he gestured that Leah should enter his tent and as she stepped past him, he closed the tent flap behind her, Jared and Ahab knew to stand discreetly at a distance, far enough not to eavesdrop on the potentially sensitive news, but close enough to be immediately available when called for to receive their next orders. The soldiers prided themselves on their discipline and loyalty to their general and their precision in carrying out his orders.

Omri stalked over to his desk and slumped heavily into his chair. Leah stood in the centre of the tent nervously, unmoving and looking awkwardly down at her hands clasped tightly in front of her. He moved some loose maps of the Philistine city around and began ordering his table to prepare for the morning war council about to be held, the routine updates and strategy discussions they had every morning.

Omri had paid a fortune in gold to several traders leaving the city for details about the city's defences and weapons and he was eager to discuss Gibbethon's newly discovered weaknesses with his men, there was a reliable rumour that there was a natural tunnel leading into the well at the city centre from the nearby lake and he was planning to send some men to investigate, find it and try to enter the city that way. If he could just breach the outer walls and get a few men inside the city, the siege could be over by that same afternoon. They just needed to finalize the arrangements and plan the minute details to signal the small group of warriors once they were inside the gates to open them for his main infantry force.

He was preoccupied with his plans and was not in the mood for Elah's petty whims today. 'Are you going to tell me why you are here?' he asked eventually, after a long and heavy silence had descended inside the tent, looking up from what he was doing, his mood was deteriorating by the second.

'Sir, Zimri, commander half the chariots...'

'I know who the baboon Zimri is!' he thundered rudely interrupting her, growing even more impatient at the mention of his wicked rival. He could find no respect or liking for the man, there was just something off about him and Omri couldn't quite put his finger on what it was, but the man seemed to have an evil air of death around him, the smell of blood seemed to emanate from his every pore, and the rumours about him were beyond terrible...

He planned to finish the siege quickly and then take care of Zimri quietly, being the newly appointed general would give him the authority to do just that, but just dismissing Zimri would not be enough. He was dangerous, the man would have to completely disappear inconspicuously because Omri didn't trust him at all and feared the worst, he knew Zimri had many spies and loyal supporters and did not want to risk an open rebellion within his ranks.

He believed that without Zimri, the men in his unit would no longer be a threat, like a dog with no teeth, they would be harmless without their evil leader, Israel didn't need a man like Zimri having any influence or power as well as loyal warriors to support him, so he would have to vanish suddenly and silently. Being the general now, gave Omri the ability and means to handle Zimri permanently and discreetly and he planned to do just that once he was back home in Tirzah.

'Sir, Zimri killed the King! He is the king!' blurted Leah before she could be interrupted again.

'What!' gasped Omri, shock stealing his voice, he jumped up suddenly from his chair sending it reeling over backwards. His face paled as he struggled with the sudden change of fate. One thing Omri did understand was that this had quickly become a very dangerous situation that placed him in an extremely precarious position. He knew that Zimri had loathed him beyond measure and would enjoy bringing Omri to his knees in humiliation or far worse...

Zimri claiming the throne would be the end of him that was a fact. He knew the monster had no respect for anyone or anything in Israel, least of all him. Something would have to be done and Abrim sending this girl to him was a clear indication that the palace staff and people of Tirzah were looking to him to do it. In a survival of the fittest world, it was kill or be killed, and Omri wasn't about to surrender or just roll over and die just yet.

The command tent was lightly furnished with a neatly made bed on one side and a large desk covered in parchments and maps in front of a chair on the opposite side, a few rugs were scattered around on the ground, but at a closer inspection, they were all frayed and well worn. It was a large tent with room enough to hold many men while in strategic military discussions. There were some chests of scrolls near to the desk and a few extra were chairs scattered around the tent for Omri's most senior men to sit on.

The silence was overwhelming inside the gloomy tent as Omri digested what he had learned in the last few seconds and thought through all the possible outcomes. Leah felt like she couldn't breathe, the air felt thick and stifling, she took deep breaths but it was not slowing the pace of her racing heart. Omri paced back and forth, his hands clasped firmly behind his straight back, deep in thought. Eventually he walked to the tent entrance and called to the nearest soldier: 'You! Get me my war council now!' The soldier immediately ran to do the general's bidding and Omri turned back to Leah and asked in a barely audible voice: 'You are sure of this? This isn't some sort of mix-up is it?'

'No sir!' countered Leah vehemently, shaking her head vigorously, she ventured a timid look up at the general's face and she was struck by how surprisingly handsome he was for his age, he had piercing black eyes, which seemed to look deep into her, framed by long thick black lashes. He was old enough to be her father she guessed by the lines on his tanned face and the sporadic grey in his black hair. He had a very muscular build and was obviously a strong warrior, he was tall and had a commanding presence about him, an air of authority. He was dressed in a dark brown, standard military tunic that reached to just above his knees showing his powerfully muscled legs all the way to his soft well-worn leather sandals. His brightly polished bronze armour gleamed and was fastened on with leather straps. He was visibly tired, she thought as she noticed the dark smudges in the olive skin under his eyes.

He was openly appraising her too; she realised and she quickly looked down at her hands once more, embarrassed by her show of boldness. She remembered that this was a man of great influence and immense power and he was used to other men being subservient to him, it would not do to have a lowly peasant woman not showing the proper respect and decorum to someone of his elevated position.

In the heavy silence that followed, Leah shifted her weight awkwardly and absently brushed a stray curl out of her eyes, her long dark curly hair was unruly and in terrible disarray after the hours spent riding to Gibbethon. Her robes were very dusty and creased, stained and damp with sweat. She realised that she must look and smell dreadful and wished she could freshen up a little. The poor horse was badly winded and she hoped that Zach could forgive her for ruining his favourite mare, but the situation was extremely desperate and there was no other way, there was far more at stake than her friend's beloved horse.

Her nervousness intensified when she looked up shyly again and saw Omri still watching her carefully, scrutinizing every movement she made and analysing everything about her, she felt so exposed, so vulnerable, but for the first time in her two-day ordeal, she felt strangely safe and pleased with herself for proving to be worthy of her Aunt Miriam's trust.

'Oh Lord thank you and please just let General Omri believe me...' she sent a silent prayer to her God for keeping her safe and free from any harm on the journey there. The roads were extremely treacherous and travel was very dangerous in the surrounding area with bandits and robbers and wild animals waiting for any unsuspecting victim to prey on, Leah truly believed that it was a miracle that she had made it to the army unharmed and so quickly without getting lost. She hadn't even seen any signs of danger along the way.

CHAPTER TWENTY-THREE

Within minutes, Omri's entire war council, his son, Ahab, whom Leah now recognized from moments before and anyone with any rank was crowded into the general's tent. The anticipation could be felt by everyone and the pretty girl standing nervously in the centre of the tent drew many openly curious stares.

Once everyone had settled down and Omri had greeted them properly, he said in a commanding manner: 'Gentlemen, there is something you need to hear.' He walked around the tent as he spoke with his head held high and his hands clasped firmly behind his perfectly straight back. 'I have only heard a small part of the message that this young girl has risked her life to bring to us, but what I have heard has convinced me that it is not a matter for my ears alone,' he paused for dramatic effect and looked around him at the men to make sure he had everyone's complete and utter attention before continuing: 'But one for the nation of Israel as a whole to decide.' As he said that he watched his men through narrowed eyes, assessing them, he needed their full support and from what he saw, he was confident that he had it.

The men all stood still bound by curiosity, silent with expectation and deep respect for their general, waiting patiently for the information to be revealed to them.

'Alright, I want the whole message', Omri commanded, 'All the details. Out with it!' he turned sharply to Leah and, ignoring everyone else in the tent for the moment, he focused on her alone, his piercing black eyes trying to dig down into the depths of her soul to root out the particulars before she even began to speak. The men in the command tent stood motionless, mutely following his example, realising that what she had to say had alarmed Omri, and not very much unnerved their general. He was always in control and confident, used to being in command and comfortable with responsibility in any situation, his self-assurance was contagious, he was a natural born leader who was revered and respected, admired and esteemed by all his men.

'Sir, my message comes from Miriam, the wife of Abrim, the head of the palace staff,' mumbled Leah shyly, she was nervous and didn't like being the centre of attention. She wished the ground would just open up and swallow her because all the eyes focused on her alone made her feel extremely uneasy.

'Miriam and Abrim are my kin, my aunt and uncle to be exact, and I live with them as my parents are dead. I work in the palace kitchen and was sent here to give you this message from them secretly and very urgently.' She rattled her story out, the words falling over one another as she spoke, her desperation and fear was not missed by Omri or any of his men.

'My aunt snuck me out of the palace unseen and then I slipped out of the city on my friend's horse. I came alone because I thought it would be the quickest and safest option for everyone involved because of Zimri's spies.' She took a deep breath to steady her nerves and then added: 'I was afraid if I told anyone else and Zimri's men found out that they would be tortured and killed and my aunt and uncle's lives would be at risk.'

Her hands were shaking and she squeezed them tightly in an effort to hide the tiny movements from the probing stares of the officers. Her head was bowed as she spoke, showing the proper submission to a person of Omri's ranking, but she raised her eyes quickly and looked straight into the general's encouraging eyes, she was reassured immediately that he believed her so far, so she boldly continued, 'The night before last, just before the end of the first watch, Zimri went into the palace, he had his entire force with him and the palace was completely surrounded. He said that he had killed Arza and King Elah.' Her voice shook as her throat constricted to stifle a sob.

There was a collective gasp as every warrior inside the tent besides Leah and Omri heard the terrible news for the first time.

'So the wicked Zimri has finally committed the worst sin of all – regicide!' exclaimed one of the men standing at the far side of the gathering.

Many nodded their agreement and all the faces were sombre and thoughtful as Leah looked around at the nations strong-men gathered before her. A loud buzz of conversation could be heard as the men all found their tongues and voiced their opinions.

'We need to act quickly!' announced Ahab and was answered with a loud cheer.

'Yes, we can't have a man like that who is rotten to the core as our king – he's a nobody, a commoner.' said a worried looking soldier.

'He should be put to death, King Elah deserves justice!' came a cry from the back of the group.

'We cannot accept another regicide as our sovereign, what message does that send? That we sit idly by while common men kill our monarchs?' called another angry voice.

I agree,' said Ahab, but the nation is going to need a strong king, and knowing Zimri…and the time he has had…he has already disposed of all of Elah's family.'

Omri allowed his men to have their say and was watching Leah intently, he was impressed by the courage the young woman had displayed in reaching them knowing the road was hazardous and the journey could be awfully difficult.

After a lot of angry exclamations from his inner circle, Omri walked to the centre of the tent and stopped beside Leah, all eyes turned to him the men stopped speaking at once, some still in mid-sentence. 'Gentlemen!' he said, 'let's not be rash, we need to explore all our options after we have gleaned every bit of information we can from our lovely messenger here. You know as well as I do that patience and careful planning wins battles and an impulsive move right now could be our last.'

Leah took a deep breath and continued, 'Sir, I wasn't there at the time, I was in the neighbouring village collecting onions for the palace kitchen, my aunt always sends me…' she was drifting off the subject slightly and got back on to the point when she realised that the general had stopped pacing and was about to say something to that effect. 'Abrim says that you will know what to do and that I am not to leave here without a message or some advice for him in return.' Leah took another deep breath as she felt her hands shake and tried to clench them to hide the tremors from the warrior's sharp eyes surrounding her.

CHAPTER TWENTY-FOUR

The silence that met Leah was deafening as the general slowly and deliberately picked his fallen chair up and sat down at his desk to think, the men around her murmured softly amongst themselves, she stood at the centre of the tent, frozen and forgotten for the moment, her legs felt wobbly beneath her; she had not slept for two days, the grief of losing her cousin was still very raw and she had travelled for a full day and night on horseback to reach them, her body was sore from the riding and she was weak from hunger and exhaustion. She swayed slightly and steadied herself looking around at the men's animated discussions.

'What more can you tell us?' asked Omri suddenly, 'Is there anything else you think of that we might need to know? And remember, even if you think it's small and insubstantial, it could be the crucial information we depend upon.'

Leah looked scared and uncertain; she didn't know much more then what she had already relayed.

'I know that no one can leave the palace or enter it without Zimri's permission and that the people are all tremendously afraid. The guards are forcibly carrying out their orders and are cruel to the people in the palace, but I was only in the kitchen for a very short time before Aunt Miriam smuggled me out of a supply door and sent me to you.' replied Leah softly so that Omri had to listen carefully to catch what she said.

Omri walked over to her regarding her closely, 'Sit down girl.' he said as he grasped the back of her elbow in his big battle hardened hand reassuringly and guided her to the most comfortable chair in the tent. 'Get her something to eat and some water.' he ordered sharply to the nearest officer. The man jumped to carry out Omri's request and was gone immediately to relay the order to a junior soldier to find some breakfast for the pretty girl with the worst possible news, news that rippled around the camp.

'Sir, also, this isn't part of the message,' she spoke timidly, sneaking another quick glance up at Omri, 'I feel you might want to know... Zimri took Abrim and Miriam's daughter, my cousin Micah, to the king's bed chamber, after he had declared himself king and the whole palace heard her screams for most of the night, they were powerless to intervene because of Zimri's men beating anyone who tried to help her.' She broke then, the tears began to run unchecked down her face streaking through the dust and leaving muddy wet trails on her cheeks, as she sat on the chair and her weariness got the better of her.

The events had caught up to her now and were threatening to overwhelm her. The emotional strain that had been kept in place with the urgency of her dangerous mission came cascading out of her in the form of sobs and she cried letting all the pent up pain and frustration out, 'It was terrible sir, the morning I left Tirzah, Micah's body was found in her bed, she had died from the severity of her injuries, sir.' Leah's voice was strangled as she spoke about her cousin; she gave up trying to be strong, she didn't have the energy left. So much had happened, so much had changed, and she couldn't hold back or stop the tears any longer, her grieving process that had been put on hold until now had finally begun.

The tears flowed freely down her face as she sobbed that Micah had been alone in her final moments and in so much pain. The girl was obviously in mourning and traumatised and the men in the tent could only stand by uncomfortably not knowing how to ease her distress while she let some of the poison out of her system.

Omri looked around at his most trusted senior soldiers while Leah cried in the chair and saw they all regarded the young woman with respect and admiration. He knelt beside her chair and softly whispered that he was very proud of her, that she had done well for the nation of Israel. Her tear stained face looked at him and he wiped the tears away gently, smearing the dust even more as he did so making a grimy paste across her cheek. 'You are very brave and have done a very courageous thing. Israel honours you Leah.' he said with genuine admiration and immediately a chorus of agreement went up in the tent as the army leaders approved of what Omri had said.

The men were all still looking to Omri as their leader and he could almost hear their thoughts, they were all thinking that the wickedness and brutality of Zimri and his illegal claim to the throne would throw the entire kingdom into chaos; it was plainly written on their faces, as easy for Omri to read as a scroll.

And in that precise moment, Omri knew what he had to do, he was the highest ranking person in all of Israel beside Zimri. He was going to challenge Zimri head-on.

- *The Hebrews divided the night into three watches:*
  1ˢᵗ watch = Sun set to 10pm,
  2ⁿᵈ watch = 10pm to 2am,
  3ʳᵈ watch = 2am to sunrise.

CHAPTER TWENTY-FIVE

When the Israelite army stationed at Gibbethon heard the news that King Elah had been murdered, all the men ripped their tunics in grief and a great cry was heard throughout the camp, the soldiers wailed loudly like children and covered themselves in dust and ashes. It was their custom to carry out the proper mourning rituals and despite the king not being very popular or well liked, it was respectful to his position as the anointed king of the ten tribes of Israel and it was the army's duty to pay the proper respects to him.

All the soldiers gathered on the parade ground at midday and waited for the official announcement from the general and his inner circle, they began to emerge one-by-one from the command tent with sombre expressions and made their way to the waiting army to rely the news formally. The disturbing gossip had spread like wild-fire through a dry haystack and the soldiers were single minded in their wish for a king that they could both honour and respect, someone who would lead them and they would willingly give their lives for. A king worth fighting for, a king who inspired them in the face of danger and would bring glory and prosperity to the kingdom of Israel once again.

They had all decided that they wanted Omri to be the king instead of the evil usurper Zimri. They knew he would lead the nation in the same way that he led the army, with integrity and honour, he was also the highest ranking person in the entire kingdom at that moment outside of Zimri's illegal manoeuvre and he was the best possible candidate for the throne, he fought alongside his men, he was a brilliant strategist and the soldiers knew he cared more for the nation as a whole then he did for himself. He had proven it often enough in the past.

Omri and his men went to address the soldiers on the parade ground and the men all cheered in unison as he approached: 'Hail Omri! King of Israel!' Men threw themselves down in the dirt lying prostrate before him. The chanting continued and the warriors yelled until their throats were hoarse. The sun beat down on them mercilessly and the heat caused the parade ground to shimmer in the red dust cloud rising from the dry parched earth. The men were all tanned dark from long hours in the unforgiving sun and accustomed to the relentless sticky humid hot weather.

Ahab looked up at his father with pride, he admired and loved his father deeply and he knew the general had worked very hard to get to where he was. He had always looked up to his father as an example and had tried to learn as much as he could and emulate the formidable man. The unbelievable twist of fate was overwhelming and he realised suddenly that if his father became the king of Israel, then he would instantly become the prince of the nation! He leaned against a nearby tree and folded his arms over his chest with a satisfied grin on his handsome face rejoicing in the sudden welcome turn of events.

Omri held up his hands for silence, he looked down at his soldiers and began: 'By now, I'm sure you all have heard that King Elah is dead.' He paused respectfully while a wail went up at the announcement, allowing his warriors to vent their rage and grief. He left them to express their outrage and sorrow for a few moments longer before continuing in a loud commanding voice: 'Zimri, the evil snake,' he spat on the ground in front of where he stood showing his distaste, 'has struck the king down and has proclaimed himself as the new king of Israel!' Omri's own indignation was evident but he struggled to keep his emotions in check. The noise was almost deafening as the army yelled and hissed their disapproval at the thought of a man like Zimri being their king, especially after what he had done and the evil omen that they believed it brought to the entire kingdom, it was undoubtedly bad luck to murder an anointed king and the gods would severely chastise the nation as a whole for the deed if it was left unpunished.

The people of Israel mostly worshipped the God of Abraham, Isaac and Jacob, the God of the Book of the Law written by Moses, as well as the Golden Calf god who sent many omens as signs to direct a follower in the paths they should take. The Golden Calf was Omri's chief god and he believed the bull was responsible for his prowess and strength on and off the battlefield. He thought about Leah and decided that she was also a good omen and a gift sent from the Calf god to him personally regarding the throne of Israel.

The shouting went on for what felt like forever and eventually when the men had quietened down enough for Omri to speak again, he gave the order: 'Men! We have a kingdom to rescue from a monster! I want to be ready to march on Tirzah at first light tomorrow!' He turned and walked briskly back towards his tent where he had left Leah eating her breakfast.

The army of Israel, pleased with the general's decision, hurried to prepare for the upcoming march home at dawn. The rush of excitement was evident and contagious and as he walked, Omri thought with a satisfied grin that the chaos in the camp was surprisingly organised and coordinated. This was his favourite part of being the general, besides the fighting, it was watching his orders being followed instantly with diligence and discipline.

The noise and enthusiasm behind him was intoxicating, he had never dreamed of being the king, and yet, without ever asking for it, he was just proclaimed king of all Israel, thrust into the throne by his loyal soldiers. It seemed so unreal to him, like a dream and he was amazed at how fortune had smiled favourably upon him. When he awoke this morning, he was just Omri, the general of Israel's army, and a mere two hours later; he was Omri, the king of Israel. He had to refrain from pinching himself to check if he was dreaming...and the girl...she was a real beauty...was she going to be in his life too?

He made a mental note to sacrifice a pure white bull and three rams at the altar on the high place in Tirzah, to thank the Golden

Calf for the blessings he had generously bestowed and entrusted to Omri once the city was safely within his control. The Golden Calf deserved a proper tribute for the favour he had shown to Omri and he was going to make certain that the god did not regret his decision to place him on the throne of the nation.

He had had no interest in woman at all since the night his wife Naomi had died eighteen years before giving birth to his son Ahab. He had loved her deeply and she had given her life to ensure the continuation of his name.

Leah definitely intrigued him and he found her courage and resolve to be very admirable, 'Maybe...' he thought, 'Maybe... she defiantly possesses the qualities of a queen.' He smiled as his thoughts drifted around the crown and the girl while he walked to his tent in a state of euphoria and exhilaration.

When he entered the tent, he found Leah passed out in the chair where he had left her with the plate of untouched food resting on her lap, and he realized with a sudden start that she had not been to sleep in two days. He handed the plate to Dan, his young attendant who had suddenly appeared behind him when he entered the tent, and then lifted her gently from the chair. She mumbled something unintelligible in her sleep but didn't wake up. He carried her over to his bed and laid her down tenderly, careful not to wake her. He removed her dusty sandals from her dirty feet and covered her with a lightly woven cotton sheet. He walked over to his desk and sat down to plot his next move. He was worried about Zimri who was extremely volatile, unstable and unpredictable, he would have to tread very carefully indeed because a wild animal was at its most dangerous when cornered, and he didn't want to make a fatal mistake or give Zimri any advantage.

CHAPTER TWENTY-SIX

The army he commanded was at only three quarters capacity and a full twenty-five per cent of the warrior force was now loyal to the Usurper Zimri! He did not want to lose any more men or put any of the innocent people in Tirzah at risk. He thought about the city and considered the civilians, and knowing what he knew about Zimri, he realised that that would be exactly what he would hide behind, the innocent unfortunate pawns. Omri didn't sleep at all that night as he dwelt on the fact that he had seriously underestimated his enemy up until that point.

He had thought it best to leave the egotistical snake in Tirzah keeping him safely tucked away from the rest of the fighting men and using his formidable fighting skills to the best possible advantage. 'Seriously, I thought that if anyone attacked Tirzah, Zimri would fight with his usual brutal blood-spilling vigour and he wouldn't be able to incite the rest of the men here or be a nuisance to me, undermining and questioning everything I say or do,' thought Omri darkly. 'I terribly miscalculated that strategy and now I have to tread very carefully.' He sat staring into the dark trying to plan his best possible course of action, making provision for every conceivable outcome.

He listened absently as the men outside changed posts at the different watches through the night and the reports were given to the rotating officers. There was never a complete silence in an army camp, sounds were muted and men whispered to one another, now and again a horse whinnied or snorted and the gentle soothing noises washed over Omri while he sat in the dark tent lit only by a single candle and evaluated the day's events, lost in the turbulent thoughts whirling around inside his brooding mind.

Early the next morning, there were no cooking fires, the men had begun rapidly taking the tents down and packing the camp up long before dawn, eager to leave and the last tent waiting to be taken down was their general's.

Leah woke with a sudden start as Omri entered the tent. 'Good, you're up.' he said briskly, 'We're just about ready march.' A young boy followed closely behind him and brought a basin filled with fresh water for Leah to wash her face with and some rags to dry off with; he left immediately to wait outside.

Omri turned to leave, stopping at the door, he hesitated and told her that her horse was saddled and ready when she was, he glanced at her and smiled and she smiled shyly back at him dropping her head in respect quickly. Omri's heart soared with that small smile from her, he disappeared out of the tent leaving the door flap to fall closed behind him and Leah was alone in the tent once more.

She hurried to get ready, splashing the cold water on her face, she gasped as the icy liquid stung her skin and she scrubbed the dirt and grime from the previous days travel away quickly. She smoothed her hair as best she could without a comb and straightened her robes. She put her sandals on her feet and adjusted the straps, wondering who had taken them off her filthy feet and how she had gotten into the general's bed. She wished so badly for a comb to fix her hair, wanting to look as pretty as possible when she saw the general again. 'Oh well, it's the best I can do under the circumstances.' she thought as she walked to the door.

Stepping out of the tent into the sunshine, her eyes took a moment to adjust to the brilliant light and she was greeted by a beautiful day and the hustle and bustle of an army about to march home.

The busy soldiers reminded her of the palace in a funny sort of way, so many people doing so many different tasks simultaneously making the movements look like chaos to the untrained eye, but it was a beautifully orchestrated symphony of discipline and Leah loved the way everyone knew their duties and went about them to perfection. She stood and watched for a few moments and wondered if she should find her horse or if it would be brought to her. Not knowing what to do, she began walking aimlessly around the camp looking for a familiar face so she could find out what she was to do next.

Men smiled at her as she passed them by busy with their duties, loading the wagons, checking the supplies and packing everything up. Behind her, some men started taking the general's tent down. She walked over to where she spotted the horses being prepared for the march back and saw her mare with them.

Zach's mare looked refreshed and fine and Leah thanked God that she had not done any lasting damage to the beautiful animal, she was saddled and standing patiently, swishing her tail to chase away the annoying flies and nibbling a patch of sweet grass at her feet.

The smell of horse excrement was dreadful because the men had not bothered to clean out the horse manure from the enclosures in anticipation of the march home; Leah reached up and stroked her horses face lovingly, rubbing gently as the mare nuzzled at her hand for a treat. In her haste to leave Tirzah, she had not bothered to learn the horse's name, and she regretted that now, talking to the horse soothingly, she checked the saddle and tried to brush some of the tangles out of her pretty black mane with her fingers.

'Mount up!' the order rippled around the army and a short while later, they were ready to leave the Philistine's territory behind them and head for Tirzah.

Omri rode his beautiful black stallion over to Leah, 'I am taking the army on ahead; you are to stay with the wagons.' he ordered, and then remembering that she was not a soldier, he added in a more gentle tone, 'It will be an easier trip and far less dangerous for you after your hard ride here.' He smiled reassuringly at her as he rode away leaving her with the wagons and two hundred of the armed warriors to travel behind the main army at a slightly slower speed.

Without the cumbersome baggage train, the main army travelled fast but even at a quick march, their hometown was still a two day ride away at the pace they were going. They wanted to get back to Israel, to their wives, girlfriends, children and families. The men wore solemn expressions and all were thinking the same thing, 'What has happened in Israel?' Their thoughts drifted from the palace to the common homes as men wondered what they would find there.

The Philistines could be seen peering curiously over the high walls of Gibbethon, wandering what stroke of fortune had freed their city. Which one of their gods had given this favour, had brought this twist of fate, because the Israelites were simply marching away! Abandoning a siege that they would surely have been victorious over if they had just waited another few weeks, by then the last of the rats would have been eaten and they would have had no choice but to boil and eat the bodies of the dead if they were to survive and continue to withstand Israel, failing that, their only other option until now had been to surrender to the mercy of General Omri and submit to the Israelite king and pay all their wealth over to them as tribute.

The cheers from the Philistine city rang humiliatingly in Omri's ears and he solemnly vowed to himself that he would be back as soon as he could with more men and weapons to bring the city of Gibbethon to its knees, and into submission to Israel with one quick fatal strike, its riches would be plundered, its women would by raped and its soldiers would all be butchered. Gibbethon would roe the day that it disrespected him and he would exact a terrible vengeance for the insult to his integrity and honour.

CHAPTER TWENTY-SEVEN

Tirzah, Israel.
The fifth day of King Zimri's reign.

The thirty-five kilometre journey from Gibbethon eventually came to an end and the city of Tirzah could be seen in the distance. The citadel rose up from the centre of the city looking majestic and elegant with its high white walls so strong and beautiful reflecting the brilliant morning sunlight. The banners hung limply in the stifling still air, no breeze could be felt at all and the heat shimmer made the city appear to hang suspended from the ground and dance gracefully in the air.

A busy hustle and bustle could be seen in the market place along the edges of the city, as the traders sold their wares and haggled over the prices of their goods. The sacred high place where the altar to the Golden Calf god stood was a hive of activity; no doubt the high priests were trying to appeal to the Calf God to aid them in these troublesome times with many animal sacrifices, blood being the most sort after commodity of the gods.

Omri's warriors watched intently from the plain as their tired horses slowed to allow the foot soldiers to catch up to them, they were all hot and thirsty, the dust cloud they had stirred up hung thick and heavy in the motionless air, coating their skin and hair in a layer of fine yellow crud and turning their spit to gritty paste in their dry mouths.

Omri held up his hand and ordered a halt. 'We'll set up camp here,' he called. 'My war council members will join me for a meeting now while the camp is being raised.' He trotted away from the main body of the army and was followed by his inner circle, his trusted advisors, the elite high ranking senior members of the army and his son Ahab. They stopped near some trees in the shade with a good view of the camp and the city below and Omri began to give his leaders the outline of his plan.

'Make sure each of your units understands that we're not to harm any of the civilians under any circumstances!' he ordered firmly, 'I will not stoop to Zimri's level by using the people of Tirzah as tools or shields. I want the entire city surrounded and under siege but I want word spread throughout city that only the civilians are free to leave, our quarrel is not with them, they are to camp on the open plain opposite from where we are camping, behind the city, I want them out of the way for their own safety.' He pointed to the hill across from where they were standing while he spoke clearly and deliberately having had the time on the march to plan his tactics to perfection.

He explained to his men that he hoped to confine Zimri and his loyal followers inside the city alone, they would be severely outnumbered and trapped with no supplies, and then they could be dealt with in a sharp but potent attack. The chariots would be of no use to the unit stationed inside the city as they could not be manoeuvred quickly around the buildings in the narrow streets, so the highly esteemed brilliantly skilled, but defiant chariot force would be crippled, Omri's infantry on the other hand would be swift and unhampered by cumbersome equipment, with over whelming numbers they would be the ones to win the battle for Omri.

He wanted the city deserted before he sent his infantry in for Zimri's head, he would lead the charge himself on the palace and meat out justice to Zimri from his own sword blade, but first the citizens of Tirzah were innocent and had to be evacuated because he didn't want them caught in the crossfire between the army of Israel and the Usurpers men. 'Dismissed.' barked Omri sharply as the meeting came to an end. His men rode back to the camp keen to relay his orders and set his plan in motion.

Omri stayed where he was on his horse looking over the plain down at the city deep in thought for some time. The horse grazed lazily on the lush grass at its feet, swishing its tail softly to chase an occasional annoying fly away and Omri sat motionless and studied his beloved capital very carefully.

Within a few hours, people could be seen with carts loaded with their possessions and carrying heavy burdens and bundles of provisions, leaving Tirzah and settling on the plain allotted to them behind the city. Omri's men had the city completely surrounded and only the civilians were allowed to leave, no one was allowed back into the city once outside the thick stone walls. Traders and travellers were denied access into town completely and were directed to the camp allotted to the city's people.

As the sun set in a dark orange horizon, campfires could be seen lighting up the plains. The smell of hundreds of meals being cooked and smoke hung heavily like a woollen blanket in the hot still air. The men that were not on duty, relaxed and muted conversations could be heard mixing into one another to become a gentle buzzing of sound. The occasional scrape of a whetstone along a sword could be heard as soldiers readied their weapons and sharpened their swords, wanting to be prepared for what was coming.

Somewhere in the camp, someone was whistling a catchy tune softly and Omri retired to his tent, exhausted and hungry. He wanted to be alone to think, eat and sleep. Dan brought him some warm leavened bread and juicy meat cooked in bitter herbs that Omri ate ravenously, he felt like he had not eaten properly in days and thoroughly enjoyed the meal, washing it down with a little sweet wine. Once his meal was finished, Dan cleared the dishes away and helped him out of his heavy armour. He stretched out on his bed and fell into a deep refreshing dreamless sleep.

CHAPTER TWENTY-EIGHT

The next morning, after the army had finished all the routine duties and the night watch guards were relieved and replaced by fresh sentries, to get some food and much needed rest. Omri and Ahab were walking among the citizens of Tirzah on the plain. They were reassuring the people of their safety outside of the city walls and listening to the nightmarish tales of the events that had taken place since Zimri's reign had begun, now only six days ago.

One elderly lady said that three of Tibni's men had taken her youngest daughter, who was only fourteen years old, from their home forcefully to the palace three days ago and the girl had not been seen or heard from since. 'It's like she just evaporated into thin air, sir!' sobbed the distraught woman while Omri tried unsuccessfully to offer comfort.

Another family told of their twelve year old daughter not coming back from the market place four days ago and there were rumours that her body had been fed to dogs outside the city walls. A few people had witnessed the horror and had confirmed the story, but most were either too traumatised or terrified to talk about the abduction, rape, mutilation and murder of the girls in Tirzah and the girl that had been found was completely unidentifiable once the dogs had eventually been chased away from her remains.

Omri honestly sympathised with the people and he could scarcely believe the destruction and devastation carried out by Zimri and his men. 'A leader is supposed to protect and provide for his people, inspire confidence and loyalty and not terrorize and torture them!' raged Omri angrily as he and Ahab walked among the people, his concern for them was genuine and the citizens could sense that he was sincerely distressed by the events that had taken place during Zimri's short reign.

The two men listened attentively to everyone's heart wrenching story trying to gauge Zimri's strengths and weaknesses within the city and offering whatever compassion and comfort they could to gain support for Omri's claim to the throne.

Omri smiled to himself with satisfaction as he realised that Zimri had dug his own deep grave, made his own bed of nails to lie in, with all the atrocities that he had committed, he might have been accepted as the king of Israel if he was not so widely feared and hated and had not terrorized the citizens, but butchering the innocent daughters of the people for a night of sick sadistic pleasure was an unforgivable act in the opinion of the entire kingdom, especially when the atrocities were committed by the very person supposed to be responsible for protecting them.

Ahab and his father found Abrim who led them over to his fire so they could sit together and talk privately. Miriam poured some spicy wine into three cups for the men and fought back the tears as Abrim told Omri of the grisly discovery he had made six days ago. He described his daughter's injuries, causing even the two battle-hardened warriors to look sickened at Zimri's handy-work. 'He is a demon!' lamented Abrim sadly, 'who could do such a terrible thing to an innocent young girl besides the devil himself?'

Omri's sympathy was sincere, he had often worked closely with Abrim in the palace and respected him immensely, his eyes searched Miriam's tear streaked face and he vowed to them: 'My friends, if it is within my power to do so, I will exact vengeance on Zimri personally and make him suffer for every drop of innocent blood that he has spilled. I promise you that on my honour.'

Miriam bowed low to Omri in gratitude and then before the three men could discuss the matter any further, she suddenly asked, 'Where is Leah? I assume that since you are here, that she reached you safely.' She looked around as though she expected her niece to appear from the direction of the army camp.

'Ahh! Leah,' exclaimed Omri sipping slowly from his cup, still trying to organise his feelings about her, 'what a brave young woman!'

Miriam looked at him quizzically, 'Yes, she is, but where is she?'

Omri looked directly into Miriam's soft eyes and told her that Leah had reached him and that she was safe with armed men protecting her and was still with the baggage train. 'I don't expect them back until later this afternoon or tomorrow at the latest.' His face was grave as he continued: 'forgive me Miriam, with everything that has happened in the last few days, I had overlooked the fact that you would be understandably worried about your niece.'

'Oh thank God Almighty!' exclaimed a relieved Miriam and Abrim together.

Omri and Ahab chatted to the couple for a while longer before excusing themselves from the camp fire and continued with their tour through the civilian camp. Where ever they went, they were met by citizens who had lost a loved one, or who had been beaten by the guards following Zimri's sadistic orders. There were just so many traumatized and wounded people, it was inconceivable that so much misery could have been inflicted in such a short space of time.

While Omri and Ahab were away from the army camp with the people of Tirzah in their temporary settlement, the wagons and siege equipment arrived back from Gibbethon. Omri saw the huge yellow dust cloud long before the arrival of the baggage train. He noticed that his heart skipped a beat when he thought that Leah was almost there and he rode from the plain on his black stallion leaving Ahab to carry on talking with the town's people and gathering as much information as he possibly could and to continue to offer relief or comfort wherever possible. As he rode towards the approaching baggage train he couldn't help noticing how anxious he was to see Leah again, and realised that, as the king, he would definitely need a queen.

He'd battled with his thoughts struggling to keep them focused on the task at hand since she had first appeared in his army camp, catching himself admiring her courage and her beauty whenever he let his mind stray. He rode over to where Leah was and greeted her awkwardly, terribly aware of the flutter of nerves in his stomach, he felt like a foolish young boy.

He had fought in numerous bloody battles, conquered countless enemies and a harmless young girl could frighten him so much and make him feel so inadequate, he was at a loss for words and irritated with himself for his inability to master his own discomfort. He had not felt that vulnerable since he had met Ahab's mother nineteen years before. Naomi, his first great love and late wife, had left a gaping void inside of him when she died which he had tried hard to fill by throwing himself wholeheartedly into his career in the military.

'Was the journey slightly easier this time round?' he asked with a cheeky grin.

She rolled her eyes skyward and had a goofy grin on her face, 'Yes, this trip was much more laid-back, the wagons were heavenly to sleep in last night and the food was divine.' She joked and giggled at her own sarcasm returning his smile sweetly, then quickly added, 'Your majesty.' bowing her head slightly in respect.

He chuckled softly and told her not to call him that yet; frowning while he explained in a very stern and serious manner that he still had to deal with Zimri and his atrocious behaviour before he could be crowned the king by the entire nation. The army had proclaimed him king, but what of the general populace of Israel? 'Their voice matters the most.' he said sweeping his arm around to indicate the temporary camp of the civilians of Tirzah opposite to them.

CHAPTER TWENTY-NINE

Leah had been surprised by the general's kindness and thoughtfulness towards her since she had met him six days ago, he was normally so brisk and business-like, gruff, efficient and professional with everyone except his son Ahab, and he seemed like a really strict and hard man, but he had treated her very gently and had been unusually respectful and considerate towards her whenever he was around her.

He had such a fearsome reputation in Tirzah, everyone had heard of the great and ruthless military general who was a genius in military strategy and fought alongside his men, recklessly brave and fearless on the front lines. Leah realised that she saw a side of him that many other people had never seen or even knew existed. Omri grinned at her sheepishly, his full lips showing perfectly even white teeth as he spoke to her: 'I know you must be worried about your aunt and uncle, do you have anyone else you need to find besides them?'

'No,' Leah responded softly, 'My aunt and uncle are the only family I have left,' her brown eyes grew misty and Omri found himself wanting to enfold her in his arms until her pain subsided. 'my father was uncle Abrim's younger brother and my mother's entire family were all killed in the same raid that my parents died in.' Leah was saddened as she remembered the tragic events of the past and the pain and losses that had brought her to this point in her life. Her sweet cousin Micah, who had treated the scared orphan girl like a sister and had shared everything with her, was now dead. Another wave of tears threatened her eyes and she sniffed quietly fighting back the tears that were making her eyes glisten and glitter prettily in the harsh sunlight.

Omri watched her closely, she turned to him and quickly looked down at the reins she held loosely in her hands, 'I…I borrowed this mare from a friend of mine,' she stammered softly suddenly feeling small and inferior now that her role had been completed. 'I would like to return her to him as soon as possible, he had the stables that housed the charioteer's horses for the army, but I don't know where he will be now.' she added hastily.

Omri grimaced and immediately realised that he was a little jealous that Leah had mentioned a male friend, 'I'll escort you in a few moments, and bring a reward to the boy for his help with the horse that has played a huge role in rescuing Israel.' he said in a very brisk tone. 'I know that Abrim and Miriam are on the plain, I spoke to them a little while earlier and they are eager to see you and are so very proud of you.' He looked down into her big brown eyes with admiration and gently continued: 'I still have some things I wish to discuss with Abrim,' her head jerked up unexpectedly at the mention of Omri and her uncle having a discussion, but he continued smoothly ignoring the curious look on her face, 'So we'll start making our way over to the civilian camp.'

Leah saw a brief softness in his eyes flicker quickly once more and smiled at him, 'I would definitely love to wash and change my robes…' she said, 'but I don't know where my things are.' She absently patted the mare she had come to love as they walked together towards the opposite camp.

'I'm sure that Miriam will be able to help you with a few things, you lived with them until you moved into the palace after all. They will have brought some of your things with them, surely,' he pointed out.

Leah smiled in response and told him that her Aunt Miriam was the most organised and capable woman she knew. 'She makes a plan in any situation, I don't know what I would have done if it had not been for her and Uncle Abrim, I owe them so much.' She looked off into the distance and her eyes began burning with the constantly threatening tears yet again, stifling another sob, she continued: 'My cousin Micah was amazing and so very beautiful. She was my best friend and I loved her so much, I can't believe that she is gone.' Omri remained silent sensing that Leah needed to talk, to purge her system of the pain, she continued telling him all about her family. 'Sometimes it all feels like a terrible nightmare and I keep expecting to wake up and everything will be as it was before. So much has changed in such a short space of time!'

Omri stopped and turned to look at her and said softly: 'Sometimes in the winds of change, we find our true direction...'

'But do the winds have to blow so painfully?' she countered smiling through the tears welling up in her eyes and Omri was struck once more by her youth and beauty, he knew for certain that he was falling for her and that she was a vital part of the Golden Calf's plan for his life, he realised at that exact moment that the girl and the crown went hand in hand, they were inexplicably entwined. He could not have the one without the other and resolved to enter into negotiations with Abrim about marrying Leah immediately.

They continued walking together heading in the direction of the civilian camp and she began opening up to Omri more about her childhood, finding him very easy to talk to, he was a very good listener and the two were enjoying one another's company immensely. They found Zach and Omri thanked him for his part in the heroic rescue of Israel. 'You did a very noble and brave thing young man,' declared Omri in a very serious tone. 'I need more men like you in my army, how old are you?'

'I'm fourteen, Sir!' replied Zach proudly, awestruck by being spoken to by the great general and possible king. No one knew exactly how to address him at this point he noticed and the thought made him feel very awkward indeed.

'I hope to see you at the army barracks early next year, you will make a fine soldier and I would like your father to come and see me after we have retaken the city so that I can thank him properly as well for the horse that was lent to Leah.' Omri winked and smiled at Leah's young friend easing the tension slightly and then the two left Zach to care for his cherished mare that had carried Leah all the way to Gibbethon.

When they approached the make-shift tent that Abrim and his wife Miriam were sharing, they were spotted by Miriam who was making a fire outside to begin preparing the evening meal. 'My child!' she cried joyfully jumping up, 'Praise the Lord you are back safely!' Miriam ran towards Leah enveloping her in a strong and fiercely protective embrace, 'You have made me so proud, I asked God to protect you and he didn't let me down!' She relaxed her embrace slightly and turned to Omri, 'Please come in, may I offer you some refreshments?' she gestured to the door of the tent as she spoke and Omri smiled at her in acceptance as he stooped and entered the low doorway, he sat on one of the straw mats on the ground and folded his long legs under him comfortably.

The tent was almost empty of belongings because Abrim and Miriam had brought only the necessary possessions that they could carry out of Tirzah in the one trip. Miriam had insisted on taking some extra clothes for Leah and the bundles had been heavy and cumbersome to carry, most of their belongings were left behind in their modest home inside the city walls.

Abrim heard his wife's happy cry from where he sat with the other men not far from his tent, he was deep in a serious discussion with the other elders of Tirzah about the future fate of Israel and what had transpired since Zimri had usurped the throne. They had just unanimously agreed that Omri should be crowned the king as soon as possible and that Zimri should be overthrown and executed for high treason and regicide. He excused himself formally from the meeting and went to his tent to greet his niece and the soon to be king properly.

As he entered the tent, Leah sprang into his outstretched arms with a squeal of delight, joyfully hugging her uncle, he was more than just her guardian having been like a father to her for seven years, they were a very close and loving family-they faced the good and the bad together, always.

Chapter Thirty

Omri sat politely in silence and waited patiently as the three hugged and after all the pleasantries and greetings had been exchanged and the men had been served cool refreshing watered down wine to drink, the two women left the tent to continue with the preparations for the meal outside and leave the two men to their important discussions.

'Please excuse the mats my friend, I mean…Your Grace, our furniture is all still inside the city.' Abrim jokingly stated the obvious.

'We are still friends, are we not?' replied Omri smoothly 'and as for calling me 'your grace', don't worry until I have been formally crowned, as for the lack of furniture, it is not your fault and I am very comfortable. Thank you my friend.'

'I am sure you are not here to discuss my lack of chairs though,' frowned Abrim suddenly aware of the formality of the meeting and the uneasiness emanating from his friend.

Omri straightened and looked directly at Abrim, their eyes meeting and conveying the seriousness of the unexpected meeting, 'I am going to cut straight to the chase, you know me my friend, and you know that I don't waste my breath on meaningless words,' he stated gravely, 'I would like to enter into a contract for Leah's hand in marriage.' Suddenly feeling relieved at having made the request, Omri relaxed slightly and took a big sip of his drink as he watched his friend from below lowered lids and above the rim of his cup for a clue to Abrim's thoughts while waiting for his response.

Abrim looked down at his hands, suddenly inspecting an invisible speck of dirt under his finger nails while he took a few minutes to grasp what had just been requested and to compose himself properly, he had almost choked on his wine but with great difficulty had controlled the impulse and eventually met Omri's nervous gaze levelly as he replied sincerely: 'I do not have a dowry for her; as you know she is an orphan, my late brother's only child.' Omri nodded and Abrim continued, 'we have raised her and loved her for seven years, after my brother and his wife along with her entire family were murdered by the Philistine raiders.'

Omri nodded again solemnly and answered quietly: 'I am fully aware of all of that my friend, I didn't come here for sheep, goats or land, I came here for a wife...for Leah. I can also understand your concern about my age, I am old enough to be her father, she is almost the same age as my son Ahab, but a king should have a queen to give him strong heirs and Leah is young, beautiful and courageous...' He let the silence between them lengthen as both men sat contemplating the future and sipped at their drinks.

'I am not exactly in a position to refuse you.' conceded Abrim eventually, 'but I do love Leah and I have just lost my only daughter, Leah and Miriam are all I have left now.'

'I swear to you, my friend that I will take very good care of her - and the two of you...' he added quickly, 'I will add your retirement to the bride-price I am to pay.' Omri offered generously, 'I admire her strength and character and believe that a queen should serve alongside the king to the benefit of the nation-I know that she will make a worthy queen to Israel...you and Miriam have done a remarkable job raising her.'

The two men were silent again for what felt like ages to Omri but he respected Abrim's right to think the matter through carefully and waited patiently. Most marriages in their culture were pre-arranged and negotiated by the parents or the family elders of the couple to seal a land agreement or a business venture between the two families.

Marriages were almost never a result of romantic feelings between the bride and groom as most often the wedding would be the first time the couple ever saw each other.

Abrim tried to think through every disadvantage to Leah marrying Omri and could find none; he knew it would only be an advantage to the entire family so he agreed to Omri's terms. Omri beamed broadly and shook Abrim's hand a little too enthusiastically before checking his behaviour and adopting a more sombre attitude again.

Elated Omri returned to his own tent where Ahab was waiting for him so that he could report the rest of the afternoon's findings to his father. Omri listened absently as his son explained more of the atrocities of Zimri to him and told Omri how all the people agreed with the decision of the army and that he should be crowned king immediately. The people were all calling for his coronation to be held as soon as the Usurper Zimri surrendered the capital to Omri.

'How many of the warriors do you think Zimri still has inside the walls?'

'There have been small groups of his men coming over to us all day long, begging for mercy and swearing their allegiance to you,' replied Ahab. 'I estimate that about two thirds of Zimri's unit has already deserted him.'

'Good! But, do not trust them. I want them arrested and put under constant guard until we have dealt with Zimri. I don't want to be attacked unexpectedly from inside our own ranks! And it is precisely what I would do in this situation if I were in Zimri's shoes.'

Ahab nodded laughing loudly, 'You would never be in his shoes!'

'Yes, but knowing an enemy is the best way to predict what they would do next, and anticipating their next move allows you to plan and prepare for it and never be caught off guard.' countered Omri seriously with a half grin playing on his lips.

Ahab went on to explain that he had already ordered Judas to put the deserters into a pen shackled togeteher until they could be debriefed at a later time and that if anyone put up a fuss, they were to be executed immediately as a warning to the others.

Omri was pleased with his son's grasp of military tactic and his leadership qualities. He was a very capable and fine young man; he commanded his chariot unit expertly and was reputed to be the greatest warrior in all of Israel. Omri was so proud of him. He was satisfied and content, knowing that Ahab would make a great king some day in the future after him.

'What are you going to do about the girl?' asked Ahab lightly, knowing that his father was captivated by the beautiful young Leah.

'Who? Oh, Leah?' Omri feigned innocence and the two men burst into laughter at his failed attempt at ignorance.

'Yes, Leah.' replied Ahab with a cheeky grin on his handsome face. 'Seriously, I've never seen you look at a woman the way you look at her. Although come to think of it, I've not seen you look at any women before!'

'What can I say? My heart broke beyond repair when your mother died...and it's been a long time...but I think I am finally ready to try again...' Omri kept nothing from his son and talking to Ahab now was helping him to sort out his own fears and misgivings. He was afraid of having his heart broken again, but was also terrified of giving up on the chance of love completely now that he had met someone who had awoken the desire in him to love and be loved once more.

Ahab laughed with obvious pleasure, 'My father, the great and fearless warrior and soon to be king is acting like a love-sick teenager!'

Omri laughed heartily too and told Ahab of his decision to marry Leah, Ahab beamed at his father, he was genuinely glad for the older man.

'You old dog!' Ahab laughed teasingly, 'you need a young woman to keep you warm at night.' he playfully punched his father lightly on the shoulder, congratulating Omri, he liked Leah a lot and thought that she would be good for his father who had buried his heart in his military career after his first wife Naomi had tragically died, leaving him with a small wrinkled pink crying bundle and a broken heart. Ahab sincerely wished him much happiness and blessings in his upcoming marriage.

121

CHAPTER THIRTY-ONE

Tirzah, Israel
The seventh day of Zimri's reign

'What do you mean we're totally surrounded?' raged Zimri smashing his wine goblet on the floor.

'Omri has the army surrounding the entire city, I think we have a very big problem,' stressed Tibni quickly, he knew better than anyone of what Zimri was capable of and was terrified as he stood there fidgeting with the expensive red sash around his waist.

'You are not supposed to think!' screamed Zimri full of malice. He hated that everyone seemed to be laughing at him behind his back at that very moment. He was the king! Who did Omri think he was bringing his *own* army against him? He stepped down from his throne and went to the balcony to look out at the plains and his breath caught in his throat at the sight.

There were tents as far as his eyes could see, he knew the army tents were the ones in uniform neat rows to his right and the civilian population of Tirzah had put up make-shift shelters in a chaotic colourful jumble on the plain to his left. His knuckles were white as he gripped the railing tightly and a bead of sweat was trickling down his face. He cursed fiercely under his breath and turned away from the scene as though refusing to acknowledge the situation would make it less real.

'We are under siege and the people have all left the city.' whined a terrified Tibni, his voice shook a little as Zimri looked at him with black cold hate filled eyes.

'Go Away! Leave me alone!' screeched Zimri at the top of his voice, he flopped into the throne and stared listlessly ahead as Tibni fled from the throne room, his footsteps echoing hollowly in the hall as his sandals slapped against the beautiful marble floor. Zimri knew that most of his men would sneak out of the city to the army when they realised that he couldn't win this war. 'No one wants to be on the losing side,' he thought rationally, it's what he would have done if he were in their shoes, and he hated them even more for it, but he knew it was a survival tactic he would have employed without feeling the slightest bit of remorse.

He sat for most of the afternoon, brooding, undisturbed, dwelling deeply on his self-pity, no one brought him any fine food or sweet refreshing wine, there were no servants left inside the palace, they had been the first to escape the city having seen the brutality of his abnormal appetite first hand. 'They are probably telling Omri about the secret ways into the palace and welcoming him with arms wide open.' He fumed loudly to himself as his thoughts grew steadily darker and more vicious with each passing minute. 'Traitorous bastards!' he muttered as he stood up angrily from the throne and began to pace back and forth.

He realised that he was beaten and decided that if he could not keep the crown of Israel, then no one else would have it either. 'It's mine! I deserve it!' he ranted, 'I took it from the pitiful Elah! No one will take it from me!' he yelled hysterically at the top of his voice, his spittle spattered from his lips as he ranted and raved like a deranged lunatic. 'Come! I dare you!' he shrieked out of the window towards the plain. He was angry with himself for getting into this situation and shouted, 'I should have killed them all! I should have bathed in their blood!'

He knew he should have controlled himself more but the temptations...the power so was intoxicating and freedom to do what he wanted when he waned without anyone to stop him was like a very strong drug which once sampled, if even only for a little while, was the worst addiction known to man. He could not resist his urges anymore then Elah could have resisted the wine. 'Think

Zimri! Think!' he berated himself and needed to devise a way out of the mess he had suddenly found himself in.

He kicked the throne room door open fiercely and it banged loudly echoing down the empty halls, he stomped out to his royal bedroom, there was a torch on the wall with the flames flickering and making the shadows dance, casting a gently swaying orange glow around the room. He reached up for it and walked over to his great wooden bed with its luxurious furs and coverings of the finest Egyptian linen and woven woollen blankets, touching the torch flames to the materials and he watched as they were devoured quickly.

The fire spread rapidly and Zimri walked to the wall hangings and fed them to the flames as well as any rugs and clothing he could find. The wooden furniture caught fire quickly and he walked from the bedroom along the wide corridors brushing the Persian wall hangings with the torch as he went.

The walls were lined with Cedar wood from Lebanon and most of the floors were smoothly polished wood too, the palace was hungrily being devoured by an insatiable beastly inferno whose tongue lapped at and digested everything in its path.

He reached the throne room and poured the oil used for the lamps all over the furniture and anything he could find, splashing it against the walls and then finally pouring a great deal over himself anointing himself with oil-he smiled at the irony of the thought- 'anointed with oil and baptised by fire!' he chuckled wickedly to the empty room.

'I will die on my throne,' he announced resolutely as he sat down. The palace was eerily quiet, the only sound was the cackling of the flames as they licked ravenously at anything in their way, devouring everything in its path and leaving only smouldering ash behind.

A wooden beam crashed down in the throne room in front of him making Zimri start at the sudden noise; he knew he would die alone in the palace; everyone had deserted him when the army had arrived and surrounded the city, abandoning him just like his useless mother had. 'They will be sorry, no one will ever wear this crown again! No one will ever live in this palace again after me!' he cursed hysterically as he waited to die

The smoke was making his eyes burn and the tears were dried before they could leave his eyes; he coughed and watched his monstrous hell fire creep menacingly closer. Orange flames with blue tips danced brightly, beautifully towards him, and still holding the torch, he dropped it into his lap.

The heat was unbearably intense as his robes melted and fused to his body and then bubbled and boiled; his screams were sucked from his throat in dry rasping gusts of searing air. The flames lovingly caressed him, singing his hair from his head, the blistering air round him scorching his beard and peeling the skin from his face, the pain was beyond words as he was unable to suck the thick heavy smoke into his lungs for one last breath, he faced death with a malicious smile knowing he had taken the palace and everything in it with him to the grave.

He knew with certainty that his final moments would burn him into the history scrolls forever and he would be remembered for eternity as the king who rid the land of a useless, pathetic Elah and then took Tirzah with him to the grave! 'No one can take it away from me! It's all mine forever!' were his last thoughts and if the fire had not robbed him of the ability to laugh, he would have laughed then at all of them, instead, a dry gasp escaped his throat as the last of his breath was sucked out of him and he died.

CHAPTER THIRTY-TWO

The orange glow on the horizon grew steadily and the people panicked at the unbelievable sight. Men and women were running around frantically with buckets full of water, trying to stop the spread of the fire to the city itself, but they were unable to contain the blaze to the palace, it devoured homes and buildings, unstoppable in its devastating hot destruction. The water evaporated before it even reached the fire making a steam that sizzled and hissed.

The heat was so extreme that no one could get close enough to douse the flames. The general population wailed as they watched their city, their homes and their belongings all burn to ashes and panic spread throughout the camp but all they were able to do was wait as the flames engulfed everything in their path, destroying Tirzah and consuming their beloved city.

The smoke was thick and black and it was difficult for the people in the camp to see through the blanketing smog. The thick smothering blue-black smoke cloud hung over the city like a cloth over a table for many days afterwards, the confusion was terrible as people looted and ran around uselessly trying to salvage any possessions from their homes inside the city. In the chaos, a young child was trampled underfoot and brought to Omri's physician by one of his men who had found the little girl lying broken but alive on the ground.

Leah busied herself with caring for the child who was called Deborah and aiding the people in any way that she could. As Omri's betrothed and the future queen, she had to uphold his honour and act with dignity at all times, a task she seemed to be born for. Omri was so proud of the way she handled herself, she was already playing the part of a beloved queen and earning the peoples admiration and respect. 'Her leg is broken, but she will heal and it should be as good as new.' the physician told Leah as he examined the frightened and bewildered child gently and gave her something for the pain.

'Thank you, doctor,' said Leah and covered the child with a warm blanket and left her to sleep. The doctor left the tent to tend to the other injured and burned people who had either been badly burnt or were suffering from smoke in the lungs and coughing uncontrollably. Leah turned to Jared who was gaurding the tent. 'Do you know how to find anyone who knows this child?'

The soldier Jared, who had taken it upon himself to keep Leah safe and protected in the confusion around the camp, peeked in at the child's sleeping form and assured Leah that he would find out if there was anyone to claim the young girl. 'I know that there are many people looking for lost children that became separated in the pandemonium during the fire, so I will ask around and hopefully find her mom or dad.' He bowed slightly to his future queen and left the tent to find the Deborah's family.

Hours later running footsteps could be heard approaching as Leah washed her hands in the bowl of water provided by Dan, Omri's young attendant. He was such a shy quiet boy and so eager to please. Leah found herself wondering about his parents too, where they were and if they were even still alive.

'God Bless you!' cried the happy mother, 'I lost her in a stampede at the camp when the fire was spreading and the people were all running around in confusion.' The woman was visibly relieved and showed signs stress and smoke inhalation and of not having slept. Leah gently comforted the grateful woman and reassured her that Deborah would be fine within a few weeks. 'The doctor says she must keep the splint on her leg for a few more weeks and that he must examine her leg before the splint can be removed, but other than that, little Deborah seems to be fine.' Leah's voice was tender and compassionate as she told the mother how the little girl had been found. 'She really is a brave, strong girl, you must be so proud of her.'

'I am,' said the woman. 'Thank you so much. I can't begin to tell you how grateful I am for everything you have done for Deborah. We appreciate it immensely. When can I take her home?'

'The doctor wants to check in on her tomorrow, and then after that I am sure she can be taken home, I will arrange for a cart to transport her to avoid her trying to use her leg.' replied Leah. The woman was so appreciative and happy that her daughter would heal that she hugged Leah tightly and her joyful tears soaked the shoulder of Leah's tunic.

CHAPTER THIRTY-THREE

Tibni left the city shortly before the fire had spread from the palace to the surrounding buildings. Omri's man at the city gate had let him out when he had bribed him with three silver coins. He had been the last person to escape the city and wondered where Omri had put all the other members of Zimri's force that had deserted their leader and had begged for mercy from Ahab when the main army had arrived and surrounded the city.

He needed to find them, Zimri's men, his men now, and defeat the self-righteous Omri. He knew that he could lead Israel and continue with Zimri's legacy of strength and a powerfully fearsome ruler who was respected and yet feared by all the people at the same time. 'Only an insecure king needs the love of the people he rules,' thought Tibni irritably as he walked around the camp deep in concentration, searching for his fellow warriors from Zimri's chariot unit.

He began plotting to undermine and overthrow Omri from the inside of his own precious ranks. He would turn Omri's prized army into a deadly weapon and then use it against him planning to have one of Omri's own men assassinate the man whom everyone was now calling the new king of Israel.

Tibni understood that he would have to be extremely cautious and cover his tracks very carefully, because Omri, he knew, was not a stupid man and probably had as many, if not more, secret agents to keep him abreast of any new developments in the army and in the city then Zimri had ever had.

Tibni saw Ahab, Omri's son with another man he didn't recognize at the edge of the army camp deep in conversation together and looking horrified at the sight of the blaze in the city. The damage was appalling and every person seemed to be in a state of perpetual shock. The citizens and soldiers were all feeling helpless as the huge flames swallowed their capital, the pride and joy of the nation. Tibni smiled confidently to himself, his small beady eyes twinkled as he saw his opportunity, to get to the father; he would simply go through the son.

He strolled casually over to where Ahab and Judas were talking and dropped to his knees bowing low, touching his forehead to the ground, 'Your grace,' he said his voice drenched with honey sweet charm, 'I want to surrender myself to you, to put my pathetic life in your hands to do with as your grace pleases.' He paused waiting for a reply and when none came, he continued pitifully, 'I beg to serve you, your grace, show you how loyal and dedicated I am to your cause, and I humble myself before one so mighty and powerful.' He waited frozen to the spot for an answer, and began to wonder if he had misjudged the young man, but then Ahab spoke and hope surged through Tibni: 'You served under Zimri, did you not?'

'Yes, regrettably, your grace', Tibni snivelled, 'but this poor man was deceived and mistaken and only following orders from his superior, as was his duty, my prince.' he hoped his demeanour was submissive and weak sounding enough with plenty of flattery to deceive the new prince of Israel into trusting him. He thought that his simple explanation was humble enough to be believed by the boy and that he would avoid being turned over to Omri himself for interrogation along with the rest of Zimri's unit. 'I would just like to modestly point out that I did hand myself over to you instead of fleeing, my prince, it should be a small token of my loyalty and devotion to you and your father.'

Tibni was afraid of Omri, he knew that the formidable general would not be easily fooled by his cunning and Tibni was in no hurry to pit himself against the intimidating man. He needed time to recruit allies and find any of Omri's vulnerabilities before he even stood a chance against the man, because Tibni knew that

Omri was just a man, and he had flaws and weaknesses just like everyone else. He just had to figure out what they were and then exploit them to his best possible advantage.

'I should let Judas take you to my father,' said Ahab warily, he didn't want to be bothered with this butt-kissing Zimri follower right now and told Judas to escort the man over to the rest of the prisoners where he would be debriefed and sworn over to Omri at a more convenient time.

While in the prison pen with the other detainees from Zimri's force, Tibni began to slyly spread rumours that Omri's men had started the devastating fire. 'Why would the exalted Zimri start a fire that would claim his own life? Omri is just as ruthlessly clever as Zimri was, but he is much better at concealing his brutality and cruelty behind his polite diplomacy.'

He looked around him at the men's uncertain and doubtful faces and took the biggest risk yet as he gambled his life on the next statement: 'I heard that Omri plans to have us all sacrificed to his god whom he worships to thank the Golden Calf for delivering us to him without any opposition. He has already offered the city of Tirzah as a great sacrifice to the bull, that's why he burnt it down, as an offering, a sweet aroma to the god.' he watched the men closely, his weasel-like small eyes glittered cruelly as they flickered from man to man, knowing that if the news was carried to Omri, he would be the one to die and there would be nothing quick about his death, he knew that they would make him suffer for days lingering in the most dreadful and unimaginable pain before the death he begged for would eventually arrive, but he continued anyway to boldly plant fear into the minds of the men around him, 'You can never swear absolute fealty to him, Omri is never going to let this stain on his reputation remain, the blot on his perfect career must be removed, he wants to erase us from memory forever and make an example of all of us.' he declared to anyone who would listen.

Tibni's argument sounded reasonable to many of the men around him and they began fearing for their lives, they all knew that Omri had no mercy on the battle field and believed Tibni wholeheartedly when he told them that they were prisoners of war at the moment instead of voluntary detainees. 'Omri tricked you all when he told you to surrender to him willingly, he plans to sacrifice every last one of us!' Tibni was adamant and he continued to manipulate the warriors and sow the seeds of dissention among the ranks locked up in the pen with him. He saw his reasoning was being accepted by some of the men around him and knew he had won them over. 'How easy was that?' he thought happily, 'I honestly thought that they might not believe me, but they are so eager to cling to Zimri's memory.'

He smiled as he continued in his most convincing tone, 'Anyone who survives this prison owes their allegiance to me indefinitely as Zimri's second-in-command, you now technically report to me!' He found he had a natural untapped talent for inspiring loyalty to himself. 'Who says that Omri should be the king?' he asked them quietly and was encouraged when a low murmur of dissent began amongst the caged soldiers, they would become the weapon he would wield to bring about a revolution and destroy Omri as he considered all his options and started to spread ideas of a secret undercover rebellion amongst the men. 'We can never hope to beat Omri on the battlefield, let's face it, Omri is excellent at what he does, and he does the art of war perfectly. He has not been beaten. Our only chance lies in using covert methods that he is not familiar with.' He smiled, he knew that that would be his edge

The men around him had been willing to die for Zimri; they were brave and good soldiers. Their unit was one of the deadliest in Israel and it was demeaning for them to be penned up like domestic cattle or sheep. 'Why should they not follow Zimri's second-in-command?' He thought with satisfaction as he asked them if they all agreed with his reasonable and rational justification and plan, then he suggested that they should all swear loyalty to Omri, just so that they could be released from the prison they were in and re-join the ranks of the army. They could then furtively begin planning the rebellion against Omri, they would secretly hit out causing panic and terror, inciting a civil war and then mount Omri's head above the city gates. 'We will meet after we are released from this cattle pen!' He hissed looking at the guards standing encircling the pen and making sure that they had not overheard any of his intricate plans.

'At sunset on the first day that we are free, we will meet at Rueben's family's tent.' Tibni gestured to Reuben standing near to him on his left, knowing that he had deliberately forced the man's hand but Reuben didn't refuse him though, and Tibni decided to make him his second-in-command, his go-to man to help him with all the revolutionary details and arrangements to be made so that they could bring civil war to Israel and put Tibni on the throne. Someone who would honour and memorialize their dead hero, Zimri and continue to strike fear into all of Israel's hearts as well as their many surrounding enemies.

CHAPTER THIRTY-FOUR

The day dawned bright and beautiful. The crisp clean air seemed to crackle with excitement, birds could be heard singing sweetly and a gentle breeze carried the perfume of wildflowers throughout the encampment.

The wedding ceremony was beautiful. All the people of Tirzah and the neighbouring villages had come to join in the wedding festivities, some people had travelled for many days over rough and treacherous terrain to witness the historic event and carry the news back to their communities in the furthest reaches of the kingdom of Israel.

Leah was carried towards where Omri stood stiffly, she was seated on a sedan chair, she had a thick dark veil hanging over her face obscuring her vision and making her totally dependent on her entourage to deliver her safely to her betrothed, Omri. She sat very still with her eyes closed as she tried to think of calming thoughts to steady her frayed nerves. 'Oh Yahweh, Please be with me…' she silently prayed, 'I am so scared, but I know your plan must prevail, help me as you use me in your will, and help me to not be deceived by the ungodly beliefs of my betrothed.' Her lips moved soundlessly on her deceptively serene face. She felt slightly more relaxed then as she took another deep steadying breath and allowed the gentle rocking motion from side to side caused by the movement of the chair to lull her as it was carried forward, knowing that what was happening now was bigger than her fears.

Abrim and Miriam walked behind Leah's chair singing and dancing joyfully along with the musical procession that made up

Leah's entourage, they were dropping flowers along the way as they sang of love, prosperity and blessings to descend upon the royal couple. Ahab stood proudly at attention beside his father in the full ceremonial uniform of the General of the Army of Israel.

The four strong guards, carefully handpicked by Omri because they were his most trusted soldiers included Jared, who had quickly become Omri's trusted advisor and friend as well as Judas, Ahab's closest friend. They approached the altar and then gently placed the chair on the ground in front of Omri. He extended his hand to Leah and she took it gingerly, symbolically submitting to Omri and accepting her husband's provision and protection. She allowed him to lead her blindly to in front of the altar and then she stood still beside him with flowers and pearls woven through her long dark hair that reached down to her waist, intricate embroidery covered her gown made from the slipperiest cream coloured Sidonian silk, sewed with the finest golden thread and peppered with sparkling jewels sewn into the elaborately embroidered delicate patterns making her gown shimmer in the twinkling light of the candles inside the large ceremonial tent.

The floor was completely covered in rose petals and the flowery scent was sickly sweet as they were crushed underfoot of the numerous guests. The perfumes from the many flowers decorating the tent along the sides was thick and cloying in the air, there were pinkish almond blossoms and lilies and roses of all colours, and Leah's favourite, hundreds of beautiful orchids.

The incense burnt by the priests of the Golden Calf god was overwhelming and the bulls locked in the pens outside were heard moaning nervously as if they knew their fate. They were about to be sacrificed on the altar, slaughtered for their life-blood in honour of Omri's chief god as an offering for his favour so that they would receive continued prosperity and blessing in the marriage and the kingdom. Leah felt as though she could not breathe and anxiously tried to steady her pounding heart by holding her breath as the waves of dizziness passed.

Omri recited the ancient vow that had been the custom of the Israelites for countless generations. 'You are my wife, and I am your husband for eternity.' He removed her veil that was encrusted with precious stones blinking and glittering in the soft flickering light, tinkling and clinking delicately together as it moved and was handed over to Ahab who stood to the right side of Omri.

He covered Leah with a corner of his cloak in a symbolic gesture to show that she was now under his complete protection, and it was from that moment onwards, his responsibility to provide for her.

The High Priest then stepped forward holding a golden crown high in the air that resembled vines woven together with precious stones twinkling in the place of grapes high up in the air. He was chanting an incantation over the crown as Omri knelt down before him bowing his head slightly. The High Priest placed the crown upon his head then sprinkled the warm blood from a sacrificial bull over Omri who remained kneeling as the blood splattered on him in tiny scarlet beads while the blessings were chanted over him. Another priest was waving a stick of burning incense over the couple surrounding them in a sickly sweet smelling blue cloud.

When the High Priest had finished his incantations and prayers, he turned to the immense crowd gathered and announced with a loud clear voice: 'People of Israel! I give you Omri King of all Israel! Chosen and anointed by the Golden Calf god himself! Blessed with the strength and honour of 'Apis'!' The priest turned with a flourish and bowed dramatically to the statue of the Golden Calf god to his left before turning back to face the onlookers, he continued in a voice filled with confidence and authority: 'Omri will rule over our nation with the power and strength of a bull and, wisdom and will of the god!'

The people roared, the sound was deafening and Omri silently reached for Leah's hand, grasping it firmly and squeezing it reassuringly. She beamed up at him shyly while they waited patiently for the cheering to quieten down so that Omri could give his very first address to the nation.

'People of Israel!' called the king loudly in a powerful voice full of self-assurance, 'I wear a crown of golden grape vines!' his voice boomed over the crowd carrying to the furthest edges of the gathering. 'I chose the symbolism of a vine bearing grapes to represent a fruitful, prosperous land!' He spread his arms wide, 'a land that can grow and produce greatness! It is an honour for me to be chosen to rule this kingdom, and I vow to make Israel a name to be reckoned with and feared by the rulers of the neighbouring realms! No longer will they help themselves freely to our hard-earned produce, our livestock, our precious people or our land!' The people cheered deafeningly yet again, the noise seemed to shake the ground they were standing on and Omri had to wait for a few moments for the commotion to die down.

'I, Omri, king of Israel, promise you, that if you are loyal to me, then I will serve you wholeheartedly until my dying day!' He bowed to the crowd slightly as they applauded loudly. 'I have forged my crown as I will forge this nation from the ashes we will arise stronger and be victorious! The crown I wear now is a symbol of new beginnings and a promise of a huge harvest to come!'

The cheering and celebrating was loud and the name of Omri was on everyone's lips as they happily chanted and sang his praises, commending him on his humility and dignity. The nation rejoiced and Omri could only smile and thank his god the Golden Calf for the favour and blessings bestowed upon him.

Leah smiled demurely all through the ceremonies and while the congratulations and blessings of fruitfulness were bestowed upon the newlywed couple by family and friends and then the feasting began in earnest with much rejoicing and singing as all the people in Tirzah took the beginning of the marriage and the coronation as a positive omen for the beginning of great and wonderful things to come.

Chapter Thirty-Five

The wedding feast was beautiful and would continue for seven days, but given to the fact that most of the people had lost almost all of their possessions in the great fire, it was not an overly lavish display. The food was simple fare consisting of soft juicy lamb and spicy beef prepared with goat's milk and cheese that was readily available from the outskirts of the town and imported for the occasion. The women in the kingdom had worked tirelessly together to cook and prepare the delicacies supplied by the local farmers for the banquet.

There was such a contagious positive atmosphere at the feast, an air of hope and rebirth permeated the mood of the citizens, expectation emanated from the ashes after the terrible death of their city and the people clutched at the optimism and enjoyed the ceremonies wholeheartedly. They needed the short break from their tragic realities and the wedding and coronation provided that brief and revitalising escape. There was much rejoicing and dancing, singing and clapping, eating and drinking as the people celebrated their new king and his beautiful young queen.

Leah was escorted to the temporary bridal chamber on the first evening of the wedding feast by Miriam and a few other female friends, she was clearly nervous but left with them obediently. The women changed Leah's robes, helping her out of the very elaborate clothing that had been imported and specially made for her from Sidon that she had worn for the wedding ceremony and dressing her in a simpler plain white tunic made from fine Egyptian linen. Miriam brushed Leah's long dark hair and tried to comfort her niece. 'Don't worry my child,' she said soothingly, 'Omri is a good man, and he obviously loves you deeply. He will be good to you.'

Leah turned around and looked into her aunt's eyes, they sparkled with tears in the torchlight and she gently hugged Miriam, 'I know you miss Micah awfully and I do too; I wish she was here with us now.' The two women embraced and Leah felt her aunt stiffen as she held back the torrent of tears that threatened the joyous moment.

'I wish so too, but she would have wanted you to be happy,' sighed Miriam gently placing her hand on Leah's cheek and smiling determinedly, it had only been a month since the tragic events had unfolded around them and Micah was killed. 'In honour of her memory, I will do everything in my power to make that possible.'

A tear crept slowly down Leah's cheek, 'I love you so much Aunt Miriam, I am so blessed to have you in my life and thank you for everything you have done for me, you never had to treat me so well, to love me like you have. You are the type of woman I can only hope to be.' Leah confessed softly, her voice filled with love and empathy for the older woman's deep and raw grief at never being able to prepare her own daughter for her wedding night, a tradition going back hundreds of years.

'We are getting far too mushy and being a couple of silly females.' admonished Miriam gently and then switching to a more practical tone, she continued: 'Now we have discussed what you are to expect and how you are to behave. You are as ready as I can make you, it is time…God Bless you my child', turning quickly to hide her tears, Miriam began to walk to the tent flap and the other women all followed her out into the night filed with sounds of revelry. Leah was left alone in the quiet tent and suddenly she was terrified. What if he hurt her like that monster Zimri had hurt her cousin?

Moments later Omri stepped into the tent and tied the sinew thongs from the tent flap firmly together to keep the door securely closed. Leah stood frozen to the spot, paralyzed her heart was pounding in her chest and she could hear the blood roaring in her ears. Her hands felt cold and clammy and she forced herself to take deep even breaths in an effort to calm down. Omri seemed to be taking forever tying the flap closed and Leah felt sure she was going to pass out. Her mouth was dry from nervousness as she watched him turn slowly towards her.

He stood still and looked at her appreciatively, taking in the ankle length plain white tunic and the fear on her face. He had been in this situation before with his first wife, so he had some experience with a virgin bride and was very grateful for that now because Leah looked frightened, like a gazelle confronted by a dangerous predator. All the women in Israel were expected to be virgins on their wedding night-at least that was their custom.

'Come here.' he whispered softly and Leah took a few tentative steps towards him stopping about an arm's length away from him. He reached out and very gently brushed a stray tendril of her silky soft hair hanging over her shoulder. She was looking down at her bare feet shyly and he lifted her chin with his hooked finger too look into her huge brown eyes. She looked back up at him and his dark eyes were gentle, she didn't see any sign of evil or malice in them and relaxed slightly as he leaned down slowly and softly brushed his lips over hers.

He looked down at her again and she seemed slightly less panicky now, he cupped her face in both his hands, kissing her lips again harder, deeply this time. His tongue pushed past her soft full lips into the silken smoothness of her mouth and he heard her gasp at the unexpected pleasure that had begun to spread through her as he continued to probe her mouth with his tongue drinking in the sweet taste of her.

His hands moved slowly, gently down her back and he pulled her closer to him until her body was pressed hard against his. She reached up and ran her hands over his back feeling the muscles under the light material of his tunic.

His lips left the sweetness of her mouth and travelled unhurriedly down her long graceful neck, pausing at the pulsing hollow above the neckline of her tunic. She sighed softly and gave herself over to the passionate pleasure of the moment, becoming Omri's wife in every possible way.

CHAPTER THIRTY-SIX

The sun had barely peeked over the horizon and wisps of mist were dancing lightly in the chill air before him as Tibni walked awkwardly in the dim morning light stumbling over the rough rocky ground. The camp was stirring around him and there were muted greetings to be heard coming from all around him as people began to rise and prepare for another day. Cooking fires were springing up and the smoke mingled with the early morning mist as the people in the camp prepared to break their fast.

Tibni made his way carefully over to where he knew Ahab would be at this hour, the young prince would be in the training yard working hard to hone and perfect his legendary sword skills and fighting manoeuvres. He had been watching Ahab practice for many days now and had quickly learned his daily routine.

Ahab was a very talented and formidable fighter, unbeaten in all the ranks of Israel's army and respected by all the experienced warriors, he prided himself on his intimidating sword manoeuvres, his brilliant skills and prowess on the battle field, he pushed himself harder each time he practiced with the sword, which was by far, his favourite weapon, swinging the heavy iron blade in lunges and parries, thrusts and defensive sweeps faster and more lethally than any of the soldiers who trained with him.

He was young and strong and when he trained the muscles on his broad chest and arms bulged under his tight fitting tunic, his skin was tanned a dark olive brown from the many hours spent in the training yard in the unrelenting sun, complementing his luxurious wavy auburn coloured hair and his eyes were sharp and intelligent, discerning dark green pools of intensity that missed nothing.

He was weaving the beautifully balanced sword through the air expertly, slicing the emptiness where an opponent should have been and he gleamed with a layer of sweat that seeped from every pore and shone in the brilliant sunlight. His muscular legs were powerful and he moved like the wind, swiftly and suddenly, slicing and cutting an enemy in a flashing blur of motion.

He was magnificent to watch and many of the warriors would often pause with their own training drills to watch him in admiration and placed bets on him as to how long it would take Ahab to disarm or subdue his current unfortunate quarry chosen to spar against him at that practice session. It was always inspiring for the soldiers to see their prince in action and unbeaten by any rival, he moved with a liquid grace, fluid movements that flowed together in a superb dance that seemed at such odds with his muscular size and brute strength.

Ahab was usually the first person to arrive at the training yard each day, he had competed a couple of drills and by now the men had begun steadily streaming in, 'Good Morning my prince!' the voices floated over to him in greeting during his warm-up session and he moved from one stance to another so gracefully that it was impossible to tell where the one movement ended and the other began. He didn't reply but acknowledged their greetings with a slight smile or a flick of his green eyes as he inclined his head in their direction.

The sun reflected off the magnificent blade, forged by the best craftsman in Tyre and Sidon as a gift to the prince from the king of both Phoenician states, Eth-Baal. The hilt was encrusted with precious jewels that flashed and twinkled in the bright light. As Ahab lunged and parried, the blade flashed making it appear to be sparks of lightning striking constantly as he moved the blade in his training drills. 'Will you look at that,' mumbled one of the men spellbound by the awesome display of strength and speed, 'He moves like a god, throwing lightning bolts and the sun's rays at his enemies...'

'I'll fight alongside him gladly.' volunteered another of the soldiers quickly while staring spellbound at the fascinating sight of Ahab wielding his jewelled sword.

Judas approached the men who standing to one side watching the prince and smiled with pride. 'You know that the Phoenicians believe that their god, Baal, controls the weather and when they see the flashes of lightning in the sky,' he said conversationally, 'They believe that Baal is fighting on their behalf. Look at our prince, with his Phoenician blade; does he not conjure up an image of the god himself fighting for us?'

'He does look super-human.' agreed another soldier quietly almost as if to himself.

'It is impossible for us to move with the speed and power he moves at and still he makes it look so easy.' The men were talking amongst themselves and continued to discuss the prince's splendid form and outstanding ability on the battle field as a sweaty Ahab finished up his morning routine satisfied that he had pushed his body past the previous day's limits. He walked towards his armour-bearer and handed the small boy the sword gingerly. 'Put her away carefully after you have wiped her down,' he said as the boy nodded his head eagerly. 'Don't drop her and be very careful, the blade is extremely sharp, I don't want you losing any fingers! I'll be in to check and oil the blade properly later.'

'Yes your majesty!' enthused the young boy quickly and wrapped the sword with an oiled cloth to protect himself against the razor sharp edges, he lifted it reverently and headed towards the tent that Ahab was living in, he was careful to carry out his instructions to the last letter and please his prince.

'My Prince!' called Tibni casually as he ran to catch up to Ahab who was leaving the training yard.

Ahab slowed and turned in surprise coming face–to-face with the man. 'Make it quick!' he snapped impatiently and continued to walk gesturing that Tibni should walk with him. Tibni tried to match Ahab's stride and was gasping for breath.

Ahab recognised the scrawny small man immediately as the man who had approached during the terrible fire. He didn't trust the sullen faced former captain and hoped the distrust did not show on his own carefully masked face as he tried hard to hide his irritation.

Tibni smiled brightly and inquired: 'Do you remember me, your grace?' his nasal voice grated on Ahab's nerves and he had to force himself to keep the dislike from his face as Tibni continued: 'I surrendered myself over to you on the night of the great fire.'

'Oh yes, it's Tibni. Isn't it? Zimri's captain?' Ahab phrased the statement like a rhetorical question. Was the weasel-faced soldier only following out orders like he claimed he was, or did he have a much darker invested interest in Zimri's murderous reign? Ahab wondered.

'My Prince, I am humbled that you remember such a lowly soldier like myself who can only do what he is told by his commanding officer.' Tibni's voice was oily smooth and carefully controlled as he spoke. 'I wanted to ask if I could make myself available for you to command in any way that you see fit.'

Ahab thought for a few moments while Tibni stood at attention smartly before him. He kept his face neutral, so as not to betray his thoughts, he was extremely wary about who he trusted knowing that the people closest to him could either make or break him.

Omri had often told him as a child that he would become like the five people he spent the most time with, so he should always choose his friends wisely. Ahab took everything his father told him seriously because he knew that his father was wise and he studied and observed Omri closely wanting to learn the secrets and subtleties required to lead and inspire men the way the great man did. His father had a natural charismatic leadership ability that just seemed to seep from him, men found themselves following Omri to their deaths with loyalty, not because they had to, but because they wanted to be led by him above all else.

Ahab knew that there was a very good chance that he was being manipulated by Tibni but decided that he would keep this enemy close and watch him carefully to learn his motives instead of spurning Tibni and possibly making him an even more dangerously devious adversary in the future. 'If he truly is harmless,' thought

Ahab, 'then I have not rejected an innocent man, but if he is up to something, and my gut tells me that he is, I have a better chance of finding out what it is if I keep him close to me.'

Keeping his voice as disinterested as possible, Ahab replied: 'I don't give my trust away to just anyone, trust has to be earned...' before Ahab had finished his sentence Tibni cried out joyfully: 'My prince you are wise just like your father! I won't let you down!'

'We'll see,' sighed Ahab while he groaned inwardly and dismissed Tibni telling him to wait for orders in the army barracks with the other troops.

CHAPTER THIRTY-SEVEN

A few months later…

'What the…?' Omri nearly tripped over the man lying motionless on the ground at the entrance to his tent. It was early, and the sun had just begun sending its warm orange rays out over the distant horizon. Omri was awake as usual long before Dan, and he smiled to himself as he thought about how he rarely needed the boy's help but kept him around as his personal servant to give the boy his protection and keep him well looked after. Dan was shy and withdrawn and Omri really liked the boy. He had no parents or family of his own; his mother had died when he was a very small baby and he was orphaned eight years ago when Dan was only two years old.

His father had been part of Ahab's squad in the infantry at the time and had fought bravely alongside Ahab. The two of them had been part of an infantry unit of fifty warriors that had held off an ambush of over a hundred blood-thirsty Moabites while the Israelite charioteers and another two units of infantry encircled the foreign attackers trapping from all sides, the smaller Moabite force was annihilated completely but not before a Moabite warrior had charged straight at Ahab from behind and Dan's father seeing the oncoming attack had jumped directly into the path of the sword shoving Ahab out of harm's way. The man had died a heroic and honourable warrior's death and Ahab had sworn to protect the dying man's son for him in his place for as long as he lived.

Omri had taken Dan under his wing and into his household immediately as payment of the debt he knew he owed to the courageous dead warrior who had sacrificed his life in Ahab's place, it was not only the custom but also the only upright and respectable thing to do in Omri's opinion and his men loved and admired him all the more for it, knowing that their families were safe and would be provided for as long as Israel had Omri to lead the army, even if they died fighting in battles in Israel or in foreign lands.

The fresh breeze was lightly worrying the flap at the entrance to his royal tent and Omri gently nudged the seemingly sleeping man with his foot. The man didn't budge and then Omri saw the blood pooled on the floor, he called to a soldier passing nearby to come and help him as he rolled the man onto his back. The soldier came over immediately and stopped short when he saw the blood on the floor under the body and the ruined throat of a man dressed in the full leather armour of the army of Israel.

'Do you know this man?' asked Omri sharply. His instincts took over instantly and he immediately knew the dead man was a message to him personally, from an unknown source. The gaping slash across the throat, the body positioned carefully to conceal the tell-tale wound at a casual glance was well planned and executed. To a passer-by it would appear that the guard at Omri's tent entrance had just fallen asleep on the job.

The man was unusually nervous. 'Yes your gr...grace,' came the stammered reply, 'Its Zedekiah, he is in Jared's body-guard unit.' The soldier continued nervously, 'He was on duty last night and fine when I saw him only a short while ago.'

'Get me my officers! Now!' bellowed Omri. He was livid that a murder could take place right on his door step, right under his nose – so to speak. 'I want this killer found now!' he roared in anger.

Leah came to the door still groggy from sleep and gasped when she saw all the blood. 'What happened?' she asked, her face was pale and her voice was shaky, she swayed slightly and grasped the pole nearest to her to steady herself.

Omri turned to his pregnant wife and in a soft voice full of reassurance he replied: 'I don't know, my love, but I intend to find out,' he smiled at her confidently as he guided her back into the safety of their tent. He didn't want his wife to see how rattled he really was. 'Stay inside for now please, my love, just until I've spoken to the men.' Leah nodded absently and sat down heavily in the chair Omri had led her to. He brushed a kiss across her forehead and then turned to leave the tent.

'What's going on?' she asked frantically, 'Who would do such a thing?' her scared voice sounded almost foreign to Omri's ears, he turned quickly and saw the tears on her cheeks. Hurrying back over to her, he scooped her up in his arms, smoothing her silky hair, 'It's alright,' he whispered into her ear, 'only a coward operates like this.' He cupped her face in his big hands and gently kissed her tears away, 'I will have him in chains soon and executed for murder,' promised Omri gently.

'Please be careful', she begged, 'A blade is just as deadly in the hand of a coward as it is in the hand of the most seasoned warrior if it hits its intended target.' Omri smiled down at his wife, her concern for his safety was touching and his heart leapt once more with joy at the unexpected but welcome happiness they shared and the love they felt for one another.

'I promise I'll be careful,' he kissed Leah's soft full lips lightly. He could hear the exclamations of outrage as his commanders and captains gathered outside and saw the dead guard at his door, he left Leah to join them outside.

'Good morning Gentlemen!' Omri greeted the senior men as he exited his tent, someone had respectfully covered Zedekiah with a clean linen sheet. 'I seem to have been left a horrible gift during the night.' He looked down at the lifeless guard on the floor at the door to his tent. His most trusted senior advisors stood in silence, baffled by the sudden and unexplained threat. 'An uninvited and unwelcome gift, one that sends a particular message,' he paused again and looked around at his commanders. 'We have a killer in our midst, and that killer must be stopped quickly. This man... Zedekiah,' he indicated the covered form on the ground at their feet, 'has served me well, he must be buried with honour and dignity and his family must be notified and well provided for.'

He was angry but he knew that the traitor was not likely to be among his most trusted officers, each one of them had been with him through many difficulties and hard times over the years and had earned their positions with integrity, they all met his piercing dark gaze levelly and he knew that the man guilty of this crime would not be able to face him head on, he definitely wouldn't be able to meet his penetrating gaze.

'I don't want word of this spreading around the camp just yet, it stays between us for now, obviously we can't keep something like from the populace indefinitely but I think we can delay any formal announcements until we have more of the facts. All we have to go on right now is a dead soldier at the entrance to my home.' Omri spoke quietly and decisively to his men, 'The funeral rites of Zedekiah will be organised and the family must understand the need for secrecy here. We have an enemy of the State roaming around freely within our city to apprehend and execute. Our only weapon at this point seems to be that we remain calm and act rationally.'

Jared, stepped forward bowing his head slightly, he had recently been promoted to the head of Omri's personal guard. 'If your Grace has no immediate need of me, may I go to the family and see that your orders are properly carried out?'

'Yes, thank you, Jared, you sort the all burial details out and comfort the family. Make sure they are honoured and tell them their son died a hero's death while on duty to the king. That should give them some small measure of comfort knowing that their son's death was not in vain, I will not have his killer passing into anonymity.'

'Yes Sir! Consider it done.' Jared saluted Omri smartly and then bowed turning to leave, he hurried along the hard-packed dusty streets to find the home of Zedekiah's loved ones.

'I am hoping that the killer will not get what he wants,' Omri paced back and forth steadily. 'I think that if this coward doesn't see panic within our ranks and around the camp, it will force his hand and compel him to make a mistake.'

The men looked at Omri quizzically; 'I don't understand.' said Judas, 'How are you hoping he will make a mistake?'

Omri smiled a wolfish smile. Human behaviour was something he understood very well and he recognized the fact that the killer would want to receive full credit for what he had managed to accomplish. Leaving a dead body at the entrance to the king's royal tent was very daring and killing a guard was not without risk so he would have had to be someone the guard knew and didn't take for a threat. Also the killer must have some sort of military training to be able to overpower and kill a warrior of Zedekiah's calibre. Only the very best fighters were chosen by Jared to guard the king and queen.

Omri knew the killer would be waiting for an alarm to sound and for fear to race through the camp, and when that didn't happen, it was possible that the killer would try again and hopefully be caught in the process.

'That will be how we will catch this pigskin; we won't give him what he craves the most, the recognition and fear that he would feed on. He is waiting for us to react fearfully and that is not going to happen, he wants to spread panic and terror around the encampment.' He explained his evaluation of the situation to the men standing before him and outlined a brief plan.

'We must just be sure to catch this pig before he gets away with it again.' Judas voiced a concern that was on everyone's mind: 'It will get more difficult to keep the murders quiet if they continue and to prevent panic if the bodies do start piling up.'

'You are right, of course,' answered Omri grimly, 'that's why time is of the essence and we need to keep our eyes and ears open. Be fully alert at all times, we can't afford to let our guard down.' He smiled cheekily at the play on words.

The men stood concealing the body from the rest of the camp and curious passers-by until a cart had arrived and they carefully loaded the body of Zedekiah onto it. 'It should look to most of the population that we were just having a normal meeting this morning like we often do at this time.' said Michael, a senior advisor to Omri.

Just then Jared arrived back and bowed to Omri, 'Sir, the family is grieving as is to be expected, but I told them that Zedekiah's death was sudden and heroic, I conveyed your deepest sympathies and explained that his unfortunate death is a matter of state security and that to discuss the details of surrounding his death with anyone would be seen as a hostile act towards Israel. The family were obviously shocked and devastated by his death as Zedekiah was healthy, but they have promised to tell their friends and other mourners that he died of natural causes unexpectedly.'

'You are terribly talented!' said Omri in a relieved almost joking tone, a few of the men around Omri murmured in agreement amongst themselves, 'You told the family the truth and have avoided spreading panic through the community!' Omri silently thanked the Golden Calf god once more for sending this young man his way, he clapped Jared on the back and smiled at the young man's diplomacy and resourcefulness as the officers all began to disperse to begin their hushed investigations around the camp. It was imperative that life continue as normal and no sign of the mornings disturbance was evident anywhere.

CHAPTER THIRTY-EIGHT

Ahab leaned against a nearby tree with his arms casually folded across his chest waiting patiently as the last of the men wondered away to carry out their orders and begin the daily duties. 'Can I talk to you for a moment?'

'Of course, my son!' Omri replied more cheerfully than he felt. He had always made time for Ahab, schooling him in the art of war, teaching him military strategy and tactics and the fine nuances of human behaviour. He had taught Ahab how to read and write at a very young age and had never turned his son away no matter how pressing a situation was that he found himself faced with.

'Father, I have something that is worrying me about a person and I want to run it past you, see what you think,' Ahab had always spoken to his father openly and about absolutely everything and Omri had come to value his son's intellect and observations. Omri was very insightful and listened carefully; he gave good advice and never made his son feel small for asking a question or seeking advice on a matter that others might have felt was foolish.

'Go ahead, son...' Omri and Ahab entered the tent and sat down in chairs around a low table. Leah greeted Ahab warmly and poured the two men some sweet grape juice and ordered her servant girl to prepare some leavened bread with goat's cheese for the men to eat while they talked, Leah then busied herself with an elaborate piece of sewing out of the men's way in the far side of the royal tent.

'It's to do with Zedekiah's murder...at least...I think it's about Zedekiah,' Ahab began awkwardly trying to put into words his misgivings and while he vocalized his nagging thoughts, he became more sure of his deep seated suspicions having substance. 'I have a strange feeling that I know who the killer is, or at least who the instigator of the killing is.'

Omri listened thoughtfully and questioned Ahab closely regarding the details.

'So this guy was Zimri's second-in-command?' inquired Omri. 'Tibni, the son of Ginath?'

'Yes, he's approached me twice now since the great fire, the first was the night of the fire. I think he was trying to manipulate me into trusting him because he handed himself over to me personally and reminded me of that fact both times, he must have known that I would hand him over to you for debriefing and I told Judas to take him to the prison pen to be questioned.'

'You did the right thing, Ahab.' Omri was proud of his son's insight. It showed he had been paying attention to all those lessons and that he would be a great leader someday.

'He seemed to me like a grovelling, parasite and I didn't think anything of it at the time, I just didn't want to be bothered with the blood sucking leech, his flattering tongue was just too smooth and so annoying.' Ahab was apologetic and added: 'I've never been a big fan of fawning and this guy was just so false that it was actually making me feel sick to my stomach.'

'Okay, but I'm not sure what you think I'm supposed to help you with son, you handled the situation correctly, he probably realised that you can't be bought by a flattering tongue.'

'That's just it, Father! He should have realised I wasn't interested in a steady stream of sweet talk and butt kissing, but then the other day a few months ago...' Ahab's voice trailed off as his thoughts converged and he realised that it had been subconsciously bothering him since the training that day a few months ago, he had known the man was dangerous, but he had been unable to focus his thoughts or recognise it until now. 'It didn't make sense at the time, but after this morning, I think I might have a big chunk of the puzzle!' Omri looked up from his drinking cup and sat up straighter in his chair. Ahab was using his gut instinct now and Omri had always relied heavily on his own in the past. Words lie but behaviour never does and there was something in this man's behaviour that Ahab had seen and…

'I think we need to find and watch Tibni closely, I think he is the one behind Zedekiah's death.'

Omri stood and began pacing around the chairs, he was deep in thought and when he eventually spoke he said: 'He has means; most of Zimi's men will naturally follow him.' Using his fingers to count off the reasons, he continued: 'He has motive, his commanding officer is dead and he would like to reach the level of power that Zimri had before he died. And thirdly, he has opportunity, he thinks he has smooth talked his way into your trust so you see him as nothing more than a grovelling idiot.' He turned quickly to his son and smiled, 'that's it my boy! You've got him! Now we just need to find him and obviously whoever he is working with so we can rid ourselves of this blight for good!'

CHAPTER THIRTY-NINE

Months went by with daringly placed dead bodies being found each morning, they were always placed at strategic points in and around the make-shift tent city. The dead men were always soldiers openly loyal to Omri and it was seen as a personal attack against the king himself.

Sometimes the bodies were left at the well in the centre of the camp, often they were placed on the altar to the Golden Calf as a mock sacrifice, but mostly they were left strewn in the streets and buzzing with fat flies and smelling of decomposition by the time they were discovered. Always, the soldiers were killed in the identical fashion, with their throats slashed from behind, a wound stretching from left to right. Omri was afraid that the person or persons following what he believed were Tibni's orders, enjoyed killing a little too much. Too often during the past few months, the stench of decaying flesh filled the air near to the royal tent.

It was becoming increasingly difficult for Omri and his men to find the information they so desperately needed to stop Tibni and his followers. No one had any idea of who or where they were. Tibni had vanished completely and no one could pinpoint where the rebels were operating from, they had to have a base of operations, but it was unidentified and it was impossible to tell who the members of the rebellious sect were and those that did know, were keeping their mouths tightly sealed.

New alerts were issued on a daily basis to all of the guards in the city and everyone was stressed out, on edge and terribly afraid because they were well aware of the nocturnal murders and that no one seemed to be exempt. There were no witnesses and no one had information or anything of any kind to identify or reveal the perpetrators and the killer or killers seemed to know exactly when and where to strike to avoid being detected and cause the maximum panic among the people.

Tibni had last been seen on the morning of Ahab's training when they had spoken months before, the morning when he had grovelled at Ahab's feet, no one seemed to know of his whereabouts at all since then, he had never reported to the barracks like Ahab had ordered him to. Many suspicious men were interrogated but to no avail. It was as if Tibni had melted into fresh air, he was invisible, an unseen force and no one knew where to expect the next dead body. The entire populace were all afraid of falling victim to the attacker and knew that until Tibni was stopped, there was guaranteed to be a symbolic death message sent to Omri each night no matter how many of the guards were on duty at any given time.

Omri had begun to believe that a rather tight and close-knit force within his own army was following Tibni and working against him from the inside, conspiring and committing these terrible acts. It was just too complex for a large number of men to carry out undetected for so long. He began to formulate a plan, one that would require all of his cunning and daring to draw the spineless Tibni personally out of hiding.

'I hope this works and doesn't end up with me dead.' muttered Omri quietly to himself while lost in thought. 'If the coward is trying to scare me or overthrow me, it would make sense to make myself the easiest and most accessible target. An irresistible temptation, because whoever is behind these killings is ultimately after the throne. Myself and then Ahab and Leah would be the most logical targets, so I had better stop this snake before he gets to them to hurt me!' Omri's thoughts were churning around in his head as he formulated his plan, he just had to persuade Leah and Ahab to go along with it.

He hated the situation the kingdom was in, not only was it being eaten away from inside, but he had to put off all his aspirations to repel the foreign invaders in his land and conquer the surrounding regions until this matter had been decisively dealt with. An unseen enemy could not be confronted, he needed to face his foe and force the weasel to face him openly but he was positive that he had eventually found the solution.

He left the tent with only a very worried Jared knowing where he was heading: 'I still don't understand why you are not using your entire guard, my king, with the threat about; you are the target and in serious danger out in the streets, they may take the chance to strike at you openly in broad daylight!'

Omri turned to Jared and explained that he could trust precious few in his armed forces at the moment, 'It is really only the men that have been killed that I can be absolutely sure of outside of my trusted advisors, of course, those men are only dead because they were unquestionably loyal to me.' said Omri sadly, 'I know I can trust you, and the fact that I am not using my usual personal guards should give us the secrecy we need to finally gain some sort of advantage and then we can defeat this gutless opponent who only strikes when he can't be seen, hiding behind the cover of darkness under the veil of concealment. We are going to have to adopt the enemy's own tactics to have a chance of victory against him, because this enemy is not fighting in an honourable way, nor can an invisible enemy be beaten with the sword.'

Jared nodded sombrely in agreement, 'you are making a lot of sense, I'm sorry for doubting you, your grace.'

'No worries, my boy, victory will yet be ours, you'll see.' Omri sounded more certain than he felt and forced a confident smile to put his man at ease.

The streets were filled with civilians hurrying to the market to trade or barter their wares. The hustle and bustle calmed Omri's nerves slightly as he walked briskly around the city, he doubled back often to be sure he was not being followed to Abrim's tent which was not too far from the centre of the city, Omri had insisted that they be housed closer to Leah, they were after all, the extended royal family now.

Omri entered the tent belonging to Abrim and Miriam without announcing his arrival first. They were surprised by the unexpected and sudden visit from the king but eagerly welcomed him and listened to the outline of his plan. He needed to get Leah to safety outside the city before she was harmed in any way and before he could take any further action. No one besides Abrim, Miriam, Ahab and himself would have any idea of her whereabouts.

'Miriam's sister lives in a small village to the north west of here, it is not too far, but if we leave early in the morning tomorrow and sneak out of the camp while you have the bulk of the soldiers called together in the routine parade ground assembly, then we can slip out of the eastern side of the city and travel in a wide arc around the area to avoid any suspicious eyes, once we have sufficient distance between us and here, we will then turn and make our way to the north west and travel to the village of Dotham.' Abrim was careful to keep his voice very low so that no one could eavesdrop on their clandestine conversation.

They continued to make their plans quietly while Omri nodded his approval sipping on the refreshing cider that Miriam had served them, 'We will sneak Leah out of your tent early this evening while the soldiers and everyone are in the centre of the camp for the evening dedications to the Golden Calf. Leah never attends those services anyway so her absence will not be noticed, and then we'll leave from here early tomorrow.'

'Please, will you take Dan with you? He adores Leah and feels duty bound to protect her for me.' Omri was really fond of the young boy and thought of him more as a son then a servant and didn't want to see him harmed in any way, 'These faceless rebels may torture him for any information as to Leah's whereabouts and the poor boy would give his life for her, he wouldn't know anything useful to them, but I don't want him caught in the cross-fire.' Omri felt helpless at the request and prayed to his Golden Calf god to keep his family and friends safe.

'We'll take good care of him, and will be honoured to have him with us.' answered Miriam quickly in a motherly tone before Abrim could object, not that she believed he would; they understood Omri's concern for the boy as his guardian and protector.

'Keep my wife safe, please,' he pleaded as he turned back and looked at the couple again when he reached the tent entrance before opening the flap. Miriam was touched by the pain she saw in his eyes and hugged him gently, she whispered softly so as not to be overheard by anyone passing by 'Remember she was our niece long before she was your wife, we love her too and will protect her with our lives.'

'I want to catch this coward and end this madness!' hissed Omri fiercely and then he stepped out into the twilight unseen, he walked around the camp for a long while deep in concentration and frustrated by feeling so impotent and having some anonymous enemy calling all the shots and deciding his next move for him. He wandered around the streets clearing his head and covering his tracks carefully, but he passed by vendors unrecognised and unnoticed in his dirty peasant disguise.

Later that evening while the entire city of Tirzah was attending the evening dedication to the Golden Calf and afterwards, Omri and his men would then brief the soldiers about the military campaign he was hoping to begin the following day. An ugly old woman slipped past Jared, who had been told to expect an unusual visitor, into the main royal tent. She had dirty ragged robes with her for both Leah and Dan to put on and spoke in quiet hushed tones, explaining to the two what they were to do.

'Put these on immediately and then walk together through the market pretending to be beggars, don't draw any attention to yourselves, no one will be looking for a poor beggar woman and her son, make your way carefully to my tent and try to make sure that you are not noticed at all by anyone and then you are to wait there for me.'

'What's going on?' asked a curious Leah. Her brown eyes wide as she took in her aunt's disguise.

Miriam looked sternly at Leah and answered softly: 'Just do what I say, and trust me, I will tell you everything later at our tent, there are too many eyes and ears in and around this tent that can't be trusted at the moment.'

With that Miriam left the tent as quickly as she had arrived and slipped unseen towards the stables working her way around to her tent from a different direction and trying not to look suspicious.

CHAPTER FORTY

Leah and Dan changed their robes quickly and were careful not to make a noise, the robes smelt terrible, like stale sweat and horse dung and Leah rubbed hers and Dan's face with some dirt from the ground and tangled her hair under the tatty shawl she put over her head. They looked poor and dejected like all the other countless peasants in Tirzah.

Listening carefully at the entrance to the tent and hearing nothing, she heard Jared give a quiet low whistle indicating that it was safe and she slipped outside; looking around cautiously she saw that everything was deserted just like every evening during the dedication ceremony that was about to finish and she hoped that they would blend into the people returning to their homes.

She waited a short distance away watching warily around her and waiting for Jared to signal Dan to slip out of the tent and join her. He came out moments later looking scared and uncertain. She reached out her hand and took his, squeezing it reassuringly and they headed towards the market place where they would pass by unnoticed.

One stall owner moved towards his delicious looking apricots on display protecting them from sudden theft as Leah and Dan passed by looking hungry and dejected. Working their way around the city carefully, they headed back towards the centre of town were Abrim and Miriam's tent was situated.

'Hopefully we will not be out of town long before Omri sends for us,' explained Abrim, 'He will only send either Ahab or Jared. I agree with what Omri is doing, he is right, you are a much too tempting target now. He fears for your safety as these killers may try to kidnap you and hold you hostage for ransom. Not knowing who you are up against is a serious disadvantage and Omri is just trying to give this opponent less weapons to use against him and even the odds out a little by narrowing the options the rebels have. This is an effective alternative to draw his enemy out and compel him to show his face, he will be forced to target only Omri openly and then Omri can smash him.'

Leah felt sick to her stomach as they discussed their plans, 'What if Omri's plan does work and the rebel is forced to take him on and what if...' Leah began worrying, afraid of losing her husband, she had come to love him deeply and her heart felt like it was breaking.

'Hush now my child!' whispered Miriam, 'It is not good for you or the baby!' Leah was heavily pregnant, and as if in answer to Miriam's statement, the baby kicked wildly making Leah's belly move suddenly under her tatty robes.

'We all know that Omri and Ahab are the best swordsmen in Israel, his plan is risky, I know, but remember my child, God is ultimately in control and His will is going to be done, whatever that is.' Her aunt's gentle voice soothed Leah's fears and she relaxed slightly and resolved to be strong and dignified and make her husband proud of her.

She began finding the determination she had felt when she had ridden to Gibbethon alone months before, she was forced to be brave for Dan's sake and to act like a queen, regal and composed. She couldn't let Omri down when he was depending on them to stay safe and evade the rebels.

'There is something I need to attend to now that cannot wait.' Omri's measured tone concealed his eagerness, 'It has been waiting for months now and I am unable to ignore it any longer.'

'Gibbethon.' said Ahab reading his father's mind immediately and was not surprised when Omri nodded in agreement with the half smile playing on his lips. 'They humiliated us, hurled insults like rocks and need to be brought into submission to us, they must be taught a severe lesson that will resound to the other nations surrounding us, Israel will not be mocked!' sneered Omri, the lines around his eyes deepened as he frowned, 'I want to be ready to ride at sunrise tomorrow and deal a quick and decisive blow to the Philistines that will bring them to their knees and make anyone else think twice about laughing at me.' Omri's voice was filled with malice and Ahab knew his father would spare no one from the city they were going to destroy.

'I will call the war council, father so you can issue the orders and ready the troops.' Omri grinned grimly at his son and nodded in approval, 'By sunrise tomorrow I want to ride and restore my lost honour and dignity.'

CHAPTER FORTY-ONE

The sun began lazily drooping lower in the sky, and the bright hot sunny day began to cool with the evening breeze that flirted gently with the leaves on the trees, the shadows were lengthening slowly outside as the darkness approached. The sound of a ram's horn could be heard echoing around the camp; the notes rang and reverberated around the entire settlement. Jared blew the shofar to call the army and the hired mercenaries to the central square to be briefed on the planned upcoming military campaign.

'I want to take a small but strong force of good warriors with me and hit Gibbethon hard and fast!' Slamming his fist into his open hand hard emphasising his point. 'I would like to take my vengeance on them for humiliating us and take only one hundred volunteers to ride with me!' Omri knew that the traitorous rebels would be unable to resist such a perfect opportunity to get to him out in the open and joining in the upcoming campaign to be close to him would be their perfect chance to kill him as there would be no way to terrorize him personally if they remained behind in Tirzah.

He knew that the guerrillas were feeding off of his uncertainty and frustration, and once those rebels left behind in Tirzah, realised that Leah was not in town, he and Ahab would be the only possible targets, out in the open and on campaign, a small number or warriors surrounding them, it would make killing him and his son so much easier to cover up as it could be blamed on the enemy forces during a battle, a honey-sweet temptation that was just too appealing to resist.

A flurry of excitement and activity rippled through the camp as the men hurried to prepare their provisions and gather their weapons. The soldiers were glad to be going on their first campaign with their new king and for the first time in many years, their king would be leading them into battle personally. They were excited and enthusiastic and would happily follow Omri to their deaths. They would lay their lives down for Omri because they knew he fought fiercely without regard for his personal safety and would bring them glory even in death. If they died during battle, they would die as heroes, lamented by the poets, their brave deeds documented in the historic scrolls and remembered for eternity ensuring their immortality.

'My plan is to attack swiftly and by surprise! I want to strike only after the sun has begun its last quarter through the afternoon sky, during the third watch of the day!' A collective gasp was heard coming from the men as they looked around excitedly at one another, fighting in the dark was extremely risky and reckless and against their custom since time out of mind.

Omri's voice resonated around the square and the men listened intently as Omri daringly changed the rules of war, the codes they had all followed for centuries, 'I want to have annihilated most of the fighting men at Gibbethon just before they would normally close the city gates for the night!' Omri fervently filled his officers in on his plan, Ahab smiled and nodded to himself as he listened and admired the ingenuity of the strategy, the sly cunningness of it; they were to attack Gibbethon with a sudden unexpected burst of violence at just before dark, before the city gates were closed for the night, when the city would be at its most vulnerable, it was unheard of, shrewd and had never been done before.

Omri believed that the attitude of the conventional warfare in their era had many areas left open to someone willing to take risks and was keen to bend the age old rules. It was war after all, who decided the procedures and the codes of conduct and who would stand against him if he daringly broke or bent the rules of engagement? He would take advantage of all and any opportunities begging to be exploited to further the prospects of his kingdom.

'Where did the rules come from anyway and who would enforce them?' he wondered to himself as he often did when he thought about all the military strategies he had been taught and trained in. 'Victory belongs to those with the strength to grasp for it; no one will tell me what to do or how to do it.'

It was a general unspoken rule that battles were only fought in the mornings after sunrise, leaving the afternoons free for the armies to gather their wounded and bury or burn their dead in their customary funeral rites. They would then rest and recuperate through the night and prepare for the following dawn when the cycle would then repeat itself until the battle was decided and a victor emerged. No one ever fought at night because visibility was crucial and torches were unreliable at best, fires could get out of control and torch-bearers would be the easiest targets to each opposing side.

There were just too many disadvantages to fighting hand-to-hand combat in the dark, you needed a visible opponent and because of the impossibility of fighting blind, it had become a custom from before history was written on scrolls, to fight in the daylight, but Omri was a man of challenging the norm, his great ideas could not be contained in the box of customary unspoken rules and regulations.

Ahab admired the way his father thought, 'They won't see it coming,' he grinned excitedly, 'No one attacks at that time of day, it's unheard of! We'll sweep through the city and destroy them all before they even realise what we have done!' The other officers looked at him and agreed excitedly that the plan was extremely daring and enterprising and the element of surprise was the very weapon that would propel them to a swift and sure victory.

'I don't have the time or the patience for another long drawn-out siege at Gibbethon,' Omri was saying, 'we've been there and done that twice before. Their walls are nine meters thick and too high and dangerous to scale. The women help the men and throw boiling water and oil along with rocks from the top of the walls and the archer's arrows are deadly accurate if we are within their range, we can't let them use their walls against us agian.' His hard eyes narrowed and his brow furrowed in a deep frown, 'Remember last time they were even throwing their own people's dead bodies down at us whenever we tried to get the siege engines close enough to the walls!'

A murmur of agreement rippled through the warriors gathered on the square. 'Let's shock them into submission quickly and give them no chance to defend themselves against us by flouting a few of the old and outdated rules and strike terror into them because they will never know what to expect from us or when to expect it ever again.' His voice rang with contagious passion and determination as he saw the victory played out in his mind's eye and he was desperate to exact his burning revenge upon Gibbethon as well as draw his hidden enemy out into the open to face him at the same time.

Omri and his men rode hard and fast, they had all taken spare mounts so as to be able to travel faster for longer without winding the horses and could split the provisions between the extra animals arriving as planned in the early afternoon of the following day.

CHAPTER FORTY-TWO

He called a halt on a hill sheltered from view from the city by thick trees and the men rested in the cool shade for a short while. They watched the gate and the random movements of the people around Gibbethon and were happy to see that all was as it should be. The men ate a very quick light meal of dried meat and raisons and the horses were refreshed with plenty of water and they munched on the sweet grass growing on the opposite side of the hill to the city. The Israelites were certain that their presence had not yet been detected and they wanted to stay out of sight for as long as possible to avoid spoiling the surprise they had planned.

There was a hive of activity at the main city gate where the business meetings were always held and the elders of a city acted as judges who decided many important matters at the gates of the cities in the entire region. Traders were hurrying to be admitted inside the safety of the thick stone walls before sunset. Being locked out of a city overnight was extremely dangerous with bandits and wild animals lurking in the darkness waiting for such an opportunity to catch the unfortunate exposed traveller or outcast. 'See they have already closed the other smaller gates to the east and the west, it is only the main gate left open now forhte last of the traders. They think they are safe!' chuckled Ahab.

'We ride!' roared Omri loudly when he was satisfied that it was late enough to be an unexpected attack, but still early enough to get into the city and leave sufficient light to see what would be going on during the violence.

A deliberate silence enveloped the men as they resolutely mounted their horses. The men were all enthusiastic about the plan feeling confident and revelling in the cunning element of surprise, they could not wait to carry it out and see the shocked expressions on their enemy's faces.

They loved the military genius of Omri's strategies and would gladly ride to their deaths to bring him any advantage. Omri kept the eagerness from his voice as he ordered that they stay in formation until inside the gates. 'Once we are all inside, spread out and kill any and all the men you can find! I don't want any male prisoners! Remember the soldiers will not all be in armour because they won't be expecting an attack until sunrise at the earliest and then they would hide behind their high walls believing they are safe!' the soldiers laughed gleefully already feeling the effects of the rising blood-lust rushing through their veins, the adrenalin coursing through their bodies turning them into weapons of mass destruction.

They rode four abreast at a full gallop in a tight solid line. Row after row of four lined up neatly leaving no gaps in the solid moving mass of impenetrable violence. The horses were straining, men were riding hard and before the alarm could be sounded inside the city of Gibbethon, the gate-keepers were killed by the men in the front line with Omri. He and Ahab rode side by side with Jared and Judas on either side of them.

The four front riders made a solid wall of horse flesh, fear and bloody death. They smashed their way through the streets, men and women were trampled underfoot by the horses as they rushed to the gates, hoping for an escape, but they were cut down by the powerful stokes of the magnificent jewelled swords Omri and Ahab wielded as panic and terror spread through the inhabitants in the city like fire through a dry haystack.

Ahab thrust his sword through a man's throat who had tried to grab the reins of his horse. He died gargling on his own blood, and no sooner had he freed his blade from the bloody mess, when it was thrust viciously into another, slicing at limbs, stabbing and cutting through flesh like a hot knife through butter. The screaming was terrible as women and children ran and scattered through the streets trying to find a respite from all the killing or a safe place to hide. It was a bloody and brutal business and the soldiers of Gibbethon were utterly unprepared for the sudden attack, running around as helpless as the women in the city they were meant to defend.

Omri gave his son a curt approving nod as they both turned their horses back to the heart of the battle. Slashing and cutting at men who bravely but futilely, hopelessly trying to defend their city in an already lost cause.

The victory was within Israel's grasp and the Philistine blood was flowing freely like a slick oily river in the streets of their beloved city.

Screaming was coming from every direction as the men charged through the streets around the city on their horses cutting anyone down who got in their way. Smoke billowed from burning buildings and evidence of mayhem and pandemonium was everywhere. Many of the Philistines were hopelessly surrendering and asking for mercy, begging for their lives and throwing themselves down at the feet of the Israelites.

When the noise of the battle had started to fade and the city was officially claimed by the Israelites, Omri heard Jared yell sharply: 'Look out behind you!' He didn't turn around as would have been expected, but instead, Omri dropped with unbelievable speed to the ground and rolled towards where his attacker would have been, he regained his feet with swift catlike grace and stared straight into a his enemy, the man's features were dominated by surprise at Omri's unanticipated move. Omri had been expecting something like this all along, it had been part of his plot and now that it was upon him he felt relieved at finally seeing his careful plan bear the intended fruit.

A relief and determination flooded through Omri that the rebel force would soon be crushed and the gruella warfare they had embarked upon in his kingdom would soon be behind them once and for all.

He faced an unfamiliar face, a man he did not immediately recognize, a man who had been at Zimri's side through everything, a dangerous man who had cunningly deceived many into following him – Tibni, son of Ginath. A group of five Israelite soldiers had surrounded Ahab, Jared and Judas and had their swords drawn menacingly held at the throats of the three men. The rest of the warriors hesitated and lowered their weapons slowly as the hostage takers threatened to kill Ahab if they didn't disarm immediately.

Tibni was seething because he was now forced to fight Omri with a sword in hand-to-hand combat. He had planned to deceitfully stab Omri with the dagger concealed in his belt as he casually passed him by, thereby avoiding having to face the legendary brute strength and skill of Omri in open combat, but now he had no choice if he wanted to keep the loyalty of his followers. He knew he was no match for Omri's expertise and stamina but also knew that Omri fought with integrity and he had no such scruples.

He bent down suddenly and grabbed a handful of the red dusty earth and flung it hurriedly into Omri's face, blinding him temporarily and using the sly advantage while they were engaged in a heated clash of flashing steel and mismatched skills. Tibni thrust his sword into Omri's side but Omri anticipated the basic manoeuvre and twisted away instinctively out of reach of the devious blade, it caught him on his armour, glancing off it and denting it just below his ribs on his left side.

Omri roared in anger and swung his sword overhead in an arc as he twirled around with a ferocity and speed that defied belief, his eyes were still partially blinded by the dust in them and they burnt and watered, grimy tears were streaming down his cheeks, but he felt rather than saw his sword hit flesh and bone and a spray of warm blood splashed into his face. Tibni thumped to the ground at Omri's feet, his head rolling away from the lifeless body, a look of terrified disbelief in the dead staring eyes.

The men holding Ahab, Jared and Judas hostage dropped their swords in surrender and begged for mercy as soon as they saw that their leader had lost his head. The warriors loyal to Omri quickly surrounded and subdued the rebels, and forced them onto their knees roughly.

'They had their chance to show me loyalty after following Zimri, and now they repay my previous mercy with this!' Omri was seething and his voice reverberated around Gibbethon as he bellowed. His rage was obvious as he gave the command: 'Off with their heads! Now!' He thundered and turned away from the scene, he signalled to Ahab to join him as he walked towards the well to get some fresh water to slake his dreadful thirst.

The five rebel men were lined up and executed by their fellow warriors who were not sorry to do the gruesome deed because of the dishonour they had brought to the army of Israel.

Omri sat in the shade under a large fig tree; Ahab flopped down beside him and toyed casually with a stick he found lying nearby. Omri, suddenly tired from the months of stress caused by the unrest the rebels were creating said warily: 'It's finally over with my son,' Ahab looked at his father and saw how tired he was for the first time, he nodded soberly feeling the heavy weight lift from his shoulders too, 'I'm so glad we finally caught and killed the cowardly snake,' he agreed quietly.

'I need you to take some men, and ride to Dotham, North West of Tirzah. Leah is there with her Aunt and Uncle and young Dan, they are staying with a relative, Miriam's sister, I want you to bring them safely back to me at Tirzah, I miss my wife already.'

Ahab grinned knowingly, his green eyes filled with amusement, 'I will ride at first light tomorrow. I will give the men a little time to enjoy their spoils,' he gestured at the men running through the streets and looting the city, raping the women and celebrating their victory. 'And then I'll organise them to go.' said Ahab confidently.

'We will all leave here at first light, the main force will head back to Tirzah and your men to Dotham. I need you to organise some troops to remain stationed here to control Gibbethon while we organise a governor for here once we get home.' replied Omri, 'Tirzah needs our full attention now that we have eliminated the internal coruuption. There is much to begin planning and preparing, it is time to reach out to Judah and make peace. I need to get a peace envoy together and convince king Asa of Judah that both our kingdoms are best served if we are allies rather than enemies.' Omri's eyes were focused on a far off place and Ahab didn't interrupt his father's thoughts, he sat quietly beside him for a long time enjoying the comfortable silence and companionship and then much later he stood and went to join Judas who was watching the men distastefully as they burnt, raped and pillaged the fallen city.

CHAPTER FORTY-THREE

Ahab arrived in Dotham to find Leah getting steadily stronger after her very difficult labour, the baby had been breach and the birth had almost claimed both of their lives. The villagers had been frantic with worry and terrified of Omri's wrath if the queen should die while under their protection, so they prayed frantically to their God, Yahweh, while the midwives worked tirelessly trying to stem the excessive bleeding after the harrowing delivery. One of the midwives told Miriam that it was only by a miracle that Leah had survived because of the extensive blood loss she had suffered. 'God be praised.' was all a relieved and happy Miriam was able to say.

The baby girl was gorgeous and Ahab was immediately enchanted with his new half-sister. He held her gently in his big awkward hands while Leah sat up in her bed delicately sipping on some grape juice and nibbling on some dried figs. Abrim was outside and his voice could be heard floating on the warm breeze into the hut as he was organising the villagers who were trying to prepare the horses and carriage for their queen and her tiny princess to travel back to the capital with Ahab and his men within a few days.

Dan stood protectively beside Leah, he had hardly left her side since they had left Tirzah. He had taken it upon himself to protect Leah and the baby and watched anyone who came near to them with a jealous intensity that tightened Leah's heart. She had come to love the boy deeply and smiled at him fondly as Ahab ruffled his hair affectionately. They were all sitting together chatting and catching up on all of the events of the past week.

'Well done Dan, the king will be so pleased to hear how well you have kept the queen of Israel safe, and now you have a new charge to protect and care for.' Dan smiled proudly up at his idol-Ahab.

'Have you decided on a name for her yet?' Ahab whispered not wanting to wake the baby who was sleeping peacefully in his arms.

'I like the name Athaliah,' Leah replied with a nervous smile as she looked at her perfect baby girl. 'It means 'God is praised' and I thought it would be a permanent reminder of the miracle of her birth since it is only by God's will that we both survived it.'

'I think that is lovely,' answered Ahab, he paused to lay the baby in her makeshift crib and took a sip of wine. 'It sounds beautiful, a lovely name for a lovely princess.' Ahab smiled sincerely.

'Thank you,' said Leah with relief flooding through her, 'I was so worried that it would not be appropriate for me to choose her name since it is the custom that the father of the child should choose the name, but since Athaliah is already a week old and there is still a few days before Omri even knows he has a daughter, I hoped he wouldn't mind.'

'I am sure that my father would prefer that his new princess has a beautiful name rather than being unnamed and anonymous for so long, anyway, he is a man who is known for thinking outside of the box and flouts many of the conventional customs when it suits him, so I don't see how he can have a problem with it.'

While Ahab and Leah discussed the events of the past week, she giggled at the thought of the surprise attack and the startled soldiers inside Gibbethon when Omri lead his men through the gates. 'He is such an amazing man.' she said proudly.

'He is, and someday I have to fill those big shoes and live up to his huge reputation, he doesn't make the prospect seem easy.'

Leah looked into Ahab's sombre green eyes as he spoke about his fears earnestly, she didn't detect any malice or self-pity, only pure honesty tinged with awe and a little trepidation. 'You will be a great king someday, you are learning from the best and you have your father's blood running in your veins fuelling your abilities, you will improve upon his legacy using what he has achieved as foundations for the great things you will do. Don't worry Ahab, you are every bit your father's son, you already make him so very proud...you won't let him down.'

Ahab respected and admired Leah and he was struck once more by his father's ability to attract good people to him like moths to a flame. Leah was the perfect wife to Omri, submissive but intelligent, a wonderful queen who loved her people and the people loved her deeply in return. He spoke with complete honesty, as he told her that he was genuinely glad that she was getting stronger and that the baby was healthy.

'Father will be so happy to have you and his new daughter back safely, his mission was a resounding success against Gibbethon. We trampled the city and rooted out the terrorists at the same time, killing them all! He is a very lucky man beloved of the Golden Calf and, if I know him, he will be planning a nationwide tribute to the god soon in thanksgiving for all the favour bestowed upon all of us.' Ahab said as Miriam entered the hut with the food she had been helping to prepare for him. Suddenly the smell of delicious roasted juicy lamb filled the air, Ahab's stomach rumbled loudly and his mouth watered at the appetising aroma.

Miriam was fusing over Leah, making sure she was comfortable while Ahab ate bread and goat's cheese with the lamb seasoned in savoury herbs. The village was in total chaos. Outside, the young local girls were sighing and swooning at the sight of the handsome prince and his fearsome warriors, the boys were all asking to see the weapons and wanting to join the army themselves and the women, being honoured by the presence of yet another member of the royal family in their midst, had prepared a feast fit for a god for Ahab and his men, he ate ravenously enjoying each tasty mouthful and washing it all down with good sweet wine.

Ahab decided to send one of his men to ride on ahead to Tirzah carrying the news of the new baby princess to Omri. He didn't want his father to worry about the delay in their arrival home as he waited a few more days, playing it safe and taking no chances with Leah's health, allowing for her to recuperate for a little longer and build up her strength in Dotham before travelling back to Tirzah with her and the new-born baby girl.

Leah was still quite weak and the villagers had been so privileged to have their queen and the prince in their humble village that they had bestowed many gifts of all kinds upon the royal family. The amount of goods they would be carrying back to Tirzah would slow them down considerably and Ahab knew his father would be impatient for their arrival.

Omri was overjoyed when the convoy finally did arrive, he lifted Leah gingerly down from the carriage and held her tightly for a long time, Miriam was holding the baby and as she exited the carriage and Omri looked down at his angelic daughter for the first time. He smiled broadly and exclaimed loudly with pride as he took in her delicate features. She was not ugly, red skinned and wrinkled like most new-borns but had a soft creamy complexion with rosy cheeks and bright red-auburn hair just like her older brother's, her tiny fingers wrapped around his large index finger and his heart melted with love and swelled with pride to bursting point.

'I…I named her Athaliah,' stammered Leah nervously as she watched Omri gently taking the baby from Miriam and thanking her for everything. Leah was afraid he would be annoyed at her break in their custom and then override her decision and name the little girl something else entirely, as was his right, but he looked up from the baby's peacefully sleeping face and met her brown eyes, she saw a glistening in his dark eyes as the force of his emotions threatened to overwhelm him and he nodded with a smile. 'I think it's perfect, it's a very fitting name for her.'

Leah sighed deeply in relief and smiled happily at her husband, she was stunned by the force of her own emotional turmoil then, she and Omri and their new baby had all come so close to certain death at about the same time, it was remarkable and she thanked her God for the three miracles He had wrought in their lives in such a short space of time.

Omri began issuing orders immediately for a huge celebration in Tirzah to commemorate the victory over Gibbethon, the crushing of the rebels and the birth of his daughter. The High

Priest of the Golden Calf god was consulted and the entire region was involved in the preparations of the colossal feasts to come and the enormous amount of sacrifices to be made at the altar of the Golden Calf.

CHAPTER FORTY-FOUR

The ruins of Tirzah, Israel.
878 B.C.

'It's been six years, my Lord, and the building is still not progressing adequately,' said Simon, the master builder, his voice was tinged with the frustration he felt, 'We are battling to rebuild after the great fire, the damage is just too extensive.'

'What would you have me do, Simon?' sighed Omri wearily, 'We have two options, either begin to build a capital somewhere else or rebuild what has been the royal capital of Israel for over forty years, there is a lot of tradition and history here. Jeroboam chose this place because of its associations with the patriarchs Abraham and Jacob who is 'Israel'.'

Simon looked around him at the temporary tent that had become the permanent home for his king in misery. His long white beard was a testimony of his age and experience and his leathery wrinkled face bearing witness to the countless hours spent in the hot sun working on some building project or other. His tunic was covered in front with a long well-worn leather apron that had pockets for tools and they clanked and clinked as he walked. He was covered in a layer of white dust so fine that it appeared to Leah that he was surrounded by white mist as he moved and the dust floated up into the air. 'I know that my lord…it's…it's just such an impossible task.' His shoulders were slumped in defeat and his lips turned down unhappily at the edges, he sighed miserably and waited for his king to speak. He had tried his best but the task was just not possible, he could not reverse the terrible damage inflicted upon the lovely Tirzah.

Leah was sitting quietly beside her husband listening to the exchange, 'My lord,' she interrupted, 'would it be so terrible to begin a new dynasty in a new city instead of trying to rise from the ashes of all the evil and wickedness that has transpired here?' she asked innocently and then boldly continued when she saw she had Omri's attention, 'Even King Jeroboam had to start somewhere and build a new capital; you have the opportunity to begin something even bigger and far greater than the very first king of Israel! And Ahab would have a stronger kingdom to inherit,' Omri smiled at his wife, his dark eyes twinkled as he looked deep into her eyes, her quick mind and practical logic never ceased to amaze him.

He leaned over and kissed her forehead as he stood to walk to the entrance of his tent. It was true what Leah had said, they had been camped on the same plain since Zimri had burned the palace and city down, the same tent, now dusty with age had become their home for the last six years and maybe it was time to begin something far greater, maybe he should bury the ashes and forge Israel into a new and greater destiny. The thought was intriguing and he dwelt on the idea for quite some time weighing his options heavily.

Simon had followed Omri at a respectful distance out of the tent still waiting for his king's answer, Omri had grown to respect Simon's opinion, he was a brilliant capable man and if said he was having difficulty rebuilding Tirzah, then moving the capital might be the lesser evil. The thought of grandeur was tempting and he would be remembered along with Jeroboam if he succeeded, Ahab could, of course continue with the building projects after him and suddenly the decision was made.

He suddenly remembered something he had told Ahab long ago, when he was a young boy and was faced with a difficult decision, Omri had simply given him the advice: 'blessed are the flexible, for they shall never be bent out of shape.' He chuckled softly to himself as he realised that he was about to take his own advice. He loved a challenge and this presented itself as the biggest obstacle yet. He needed to build a strong political foundation for his newly reborn kingdom.

'I will assemble a scouting party to ride and we will begin searching for a suitable new site,' proclaimed Omri, 'In the meantime, stop all work on Tirzah, there's no use doing anything here if we are going to abandon the ruins and move on to somewhere else.' Omri ordered thoughtfully, dismissing Simon.

'Your will, my lord.' was the relieved reply as Simon bowed low to Omri and turned to leave, hurrying to halt the futile and hopeless construction work that he had believed was pointless from the very beginning.

The sound of hammers could be heard adding to the cacophony of noise from the construction sites all over the city. Men were chiselling away at the ruined and blackened stones and breaking down weakened and badly damaged walls that were beyond repair. The dust hung thick and heavy like an orange veil; there was no trace of wind, not even the slightest whiff of a breeze to cool the sweat on the men's naked chests and backs that caked in a thick layer of muddied dust. The heat was unbearable, making everything clammy with sweat and gritty with fine dust while appearing to move unnaturally around in the golden cloud as Simon hurried over to his apprentice.

'Stop all work on the reconstruction!' He ordered and immediately relieved hammers fell to the ground. The noise died down to a din that slowly became a silence and then a loud happy cheer went up from the workers as Simon filled them in on the latest orders and wishes of their king.

CHAPTER FORTY-FIVE

Samaria, Israel
879 B.C.

Omri bought a hill from Shemer for two talents of silver and began building a new capital city called Samaria immediately. He named the future capital of his kingdom after the man who had sold the hill to him.

The scenery was stunningly beautiful and the countryside was gorgeous, luscious and fertile. The name Samaria embodied the spirit of new beginnings and beauty and was itself symbolic, literally meaning 'Wreath' as the crown of a nation, the crown of his empire. An empire that he would continue to forge in bold strength and integrity and bloodshed. He was ambitious, driven and ruthless and his plans for Israel were tremendously awe-inspiring.

The hill was situated at the cross-roads of major trade-routes and Omri had begun charging a toll to traders and travellers entering or leaving Samaria on the roads for their use in his kingdom from the moment he had begun the city's construction. He quickly made a vast fortune and in return for the toll paid, the traveller was assured safe travel through Israel free from harassment of thieves and bandits.

Many more men were employed to police the streets in and around Samaria and keep them free from crime and the city quickly saw the benefits of Omri's shrewd and meticulous rule as the previous poverty was alleviated and hardships were wiped from memory.

Anyone who refused to pay the road tolls were refused entry into his kingdom and not allowed to travel any further. Their goods were confiscated and they were turned away penniless to spread the word that Omri of Israel was not a king to be taken lightly.

He became very well-known and feared quickly throughout the entire surrounding region, not just in Israel, but in the surrounding kingdoms too, he received tribute from all the neighbouring nations that he had defeated in battle or who had simply surrendered to him in fear of being attacked and destroyed, and Israel prospered like never before. The people loved Omri for the wealth and security he brought to them and the kingdom of Israel.

Omri held a special sacrificial ceremony that involved the slaughter of over one hundred and fifty perfectly bred bulls to invoke the Golden Calf god to watch over his newly established capital and bestow the bull god's eternal protection, blessing and favour upon Samaria.

He was extremely pleased with himself, as he reflected on all of his accomplishments over the past six years. He had become the king of Israel, outwitted a dangerous opponent and stopped a civil war, he'd subdued all the nations surrounding Israel, bringing them into submission to him and he had brokered a peace treaty with King Asa of Judah. He had a beautiful young wife that he adored, a five-year old daughter and a strong, very capable son to inherit his kingdom after him, he had laid the foundations for a solid dynasty and had begun to build the new capital to crown his kingdom and his reign with everlasting magnificence and grandeur.

It would be a wonder of marble and ivory, cedar and gold and the word of his city's superior splendour would spread far and wide. Omri was filled with pride and satisfaction at what he had achieved knowing that the future would be even greater than the past. He was enthusiastic and positive about the continuation of his legacy and securing the success of his dynasty.

The city of Samaria grew steadily each day as the building continued. A project the size of the one now taken on by the

Israelites was going to take many years to build, but there were a few structures already complete and Omri had moved into a section of the palace that was finished with his wife, son and little daughter while the builders worked busily around them.

CHAPTER FORTY-SIX

'Your Majesty!' called Jared, as he entered the dining hall early one morning.

'Speak Jared.' Omri was reclining on an ornately cushioned low chair eating his breakfast with Leah, Athaliah and Ahab. The king was leaning on his elbow comfortably stretched out but looked up at the head of his personal guard and friend and knew that Jared would not have bothered him at this hour if it was not immediately urgent. Omri had a routine; he broke his fast early each morning with his family before attending to the demanding daily obligations of his firm but fair rule.

'My lord, there is a very large caravan approaching from the eastern road.' Jared was excited as he brought the reports from the scouts to Omri that morning. He was an honest and respectable young man and had proven himself repeatedly to Omri in the past six years that he had held the position of the chief personal guard to the royal family, and he prided himself with the fact that he had first-hand knowledge of everything that happened in and around Samaria.

'Your grace, there is also a mysterious traveller here to see you, he came with the caravan from Sidon, he says he is the High Priest and king there.'

'I will see him immediately; escort him into the throne room and I will meet you there.' Leah stood to leave and as she did so, little Athaliah followed her out of the dining hall skipping excitedly and squealing with delight as she chased a cat down the wide corridor towards her mother's chambers, her little footsteps ringing loudly as she ran. Leah smiled indulgently at Miriam who was waiting patiently for her niece in her royal suite. She delighted in the daily visits from her aunt and the two would sit together happily and chat quietly for hours while working on their embroidery projects. Athaliah played nearby and was fussed over constantly by her nurses and all of the palace staff.

Jared showed the unusual Phoenician traveller into the throne room and led him to where Omri sat majestically on his impressive throne. He was very suspicious of the weird looking man who had a strange air about him, he knew very little about the Phoenician's except that they practiced in magic and their beliefs and customs were alien to the Israelites. He wanted to keep a very close eye on this peculiar man and he tried to hide his agitation. He would not allow any harm to come to his beloved king or country and was ready to strike at the first hint of a threat to Omri or Ahab.

Omri's throne was extremely imposing, he had commissioned one of the best craftsmen from Lebanon to carve it out of solid cedar wood and had it inlaid with both ivory and gold. The arm rests of the royal chair were the backs of two huge lions standing parallel on either side of where Omri sat comfortably on a luxuriously soft purple cushion, the lion's heads were facing forward looking fearsomely imposing and staring out at whoever knelt before the throne. Their cold menacing eyes were made from sparkling yellow diamonds and their legs were the legs of the throne itself, it was beautifully carved, realistic looking, the feet of the throne were the two lion's paws and their sharp claws were made from the creamiest ivory. The two lion's tails rose up along the back of the chair and framed the sides of the throne meeting high above Omri's head, giving the appearance that he was seated on a cushion suspended between the two huge frightening beasts, surrounded completely and protected by the strong magnificent creatures that symbolised strength, power, royalty and dominion.

Ahab sat proudly on a plain but comfortable chair to the right of Omri and watched curiously as the odd looking man drew nearer to them. He was present at all of Omri's royal duties and business dealings as they both knew it was the best training Ahab could ever hope to receive and Omri also relied heavily upon Ahab for his intelligence, insight and sound advice.

'Your majesty, I present King Eth-Baal of Sidon, one of the four main centres of the lands of Phoenicia.' announced Jared with a dramatic flourish as he introduced the man and led the stranger towards the throne. The Phoenician bowed low and touched his forehead to the marble floor in reverence at the foot of the steps in front of Omri's throne. 'Arise, my brother,' Omri's face betrayed no emotion or hint of his thoughts at all his tone was commanding and domineering.

The man rose stiffly and looked almost defiantly straight up at Omri. His hooked nose was the most prominent feature in his large bony face, which seemed at odds with his small skinny body, his head was clean-shaven and covered in tattoos and his beard was long and pointy and grey. His eyes were dark, they appeared to be black empty pits in his face and dark circles ringed them giving the man an air of death and decay. Omri sat silently evaluating the strange looking man while he waited for the reason for the sudden and unexpected royal visit.

'You should have sent messengers ahead to announce your intended arrival; we could have prepared for your visit properly and welcomed a king of Phoenicia with all the correct decorum and protocols.' Omri spoke harshly struggling to control his irritation as he sat looking down at the man who had flouted the customs and etiquettes of both of their regions.

'Your majesty,' the Phoenician began in what seemed to be a rasping whisper, Omri and Ahab both leaned forward simultaneously and had to listen very carefully as the visitor's words hissed from his small mean mouth. 'I humbly beg your forgiveness.' Eth-Baal looked slyly around the massive throne room at the wealth openly displayed there and his eyes came to rest upon a relief that depicted the recent destruction and devastation of Gibbethon. Omri had ordered that that particular artwork be carved from ivory and placed on the wall nearest to him because he wanted everyone who saw it to be aware of the consequences of rashly insulting him. The stranger stared at the scene of the slaughter and Omri's decisive victorious blow to the Philistines openly for what felt like ages, the silence in the big hall was deafening as each man waited for the other to speak first.

Omri sat comfortably, confident that his reputation preceded him and that Eth-Baal would be awe-struck by the many successful deeds depicted around the walls of the large throne room. He felt rather then saw that he had gained the advantage in their meeting as the sudden and unannounced visit should have been advantageous to the Phoenician by catching Omri by surprise and throwing him off his guard, instead, the tide had turned in Omri's favour as the stranger stood staring at the successful exploits of Israel.

Omri had gained possession of Madaba in the northern section of the plain north of Arnon after a series of skirmishes with the inhabitants there. They had surrendered instead of facing Israel's military might in a full-blown campaign that would have otherwise ended in their total annihilation.

Omri's successes in the southern Transjordan were the result of a policy of mending quarrels and establishing peaceful relations in the north and south. He was well-liked and respected for being fair in judgements and staying true to his word. He was very quick to mete out punishment were necessary but he was also merciful when the need arose.

He ended the prolonged war between Judah and Israel, it was the first time in fifty-one years that the two kingdoms had been at peace with one another, they had been constantly warring since the kingdom had split into two parts in 930 B.C.

He had subdued and conquered all the nations around him and brought great prosperity and peace to Israel from the tribute received. The entire kingdom lived in harmony and was content under Omri's rule after the poverty and blood-shed they had experienced under King and the atrocities they had survived during the seven-day rule of Zimri.

There were many reliefs depicting the different battles Israel had recently fought, some showed the Moabites paying huge amounts of tribute to Israel with their king kneeling in supplication before Omri's throne. His accomplishments were already legendary and often beyond belief. Many kings wanted insight to the secret to his sudden successes, he had brought a starving kingdom at the brink of civil war to the height of prosperity and unity in less than seven years and many would never have believed it were ever possible if they had not personally witnessed the transformation themselves.

CHAPTER FORTY-SEVEN

Omri studied Eth-Baal closely, his behaviour told him that Eth-Baal was a devious, dishonest and evil character and should not be trusted or underestimated. He knew from his many spies in and around Phoenicia that the man was wickedly dangerous and deceptive, but it was the first time the two had personally come face to face. He also knew that it was not Eth-Baal's first visit to a king of Israel, the man had been very busy trying to get his bony long claws into Elah before Elah was slain by Zimri and Omri didn't want to be fooled by the man's oily-smooth, slick personality.

The Phoenician eventually spoke, his voice was a poised and charming hiss but his eyes were dark and evil. 'I am here to seek a trade agreement between our two nations that will…obviously… be beneficial to both of us.' Omri leaned forward again slightly and listened attentively, aware that Phoenicia consisted of independent port cities along the northern sea-coast of Israel.

He was conscious of the potential benefits to having Phoenicia as an ally and securing a trade pact with them. They would act as a buffer state and slow any possible advancing invaders down from across the sea. The Phoenicians exported their cedar and pine as well as their popular purple dye and were the dominant sea traders in the Mediterranean, Omri had wanted to break into that market and increase his kingdoms economy there for a while now and it seemed the opportunity had come to him at last, literally.

'Your lands are presently hit by a serious draught and famine is widespread throughout your kingdom, am I right?' Omri asked harshly, getting straight to the point. 'So in return for…' he opened his arms in a gesture that appeared to be a dismissive shrug, 'You are in need of wheat, barley, figs and olive oil from us...yes, but what can you offer to Israel in return?'

Omri sat back in his throne casually, relaxing comfortably, he knew the Phoenician's needs were far greater than his own and he didn't want to show his own eagerness at this point of the negotiations and in so doing, weaken Israel's bargaining position. Ahab looked over at his father curiously and Omri sternly stared straight down at the Phoenician.

'Your majesty, we will bring cedar and pine, we can discount the rates on the price of the purple dye and we will ally ourselves with you in any military matters if you agree to trade with us. It is true what you say, our lands have been hit very hard by famine and we need to import food urgently to feed our starving people.'

Omri knew he had him right where he wanted him. He tried to look nonchalant as he queried, 'What guarantee will Israel have of this agreement? We feed your people and when they have grown strong on our food, you forget our pact and turn against us in battle once again. Our kingdoms have been fighting since the time of the great Exodus. No, I think...we don't need wood and dye as badly as you think, my brother.' Omri let his scorn fill the room as the Phoenician mumbled what sounded like a hissed curse under his breath.

'Speak up!' ordered Ahab sharply taking his lead from his father, realising what Omri was up to and that Israel had a huge advantage over Phoenicia at this point.

'I mean no disrespect, my good prince, I only said that I have a very beautiful daughter, beloved of the god Baal, she is young and extremely lovely in manner and form. The people in my kingdom all say she must be the daughter of a goddess for her beauty is famed throughout not only Sidon, but the entire four major centres of Phoenicia. All the great nobles and their sons have come to seek her hand in marriage, but I offer her humbly to you, your grace, as the seal on our peaceful alliance and trade agreement, the guarantee that you say you seek.'

Ahab looked to his father who remained still, staring at Eth-Baal thoughtfully, he was as yet, still unmarried and knew that as the prince of Israel, he would have to marry to further the interests of the kingdom instead of for love. He had accepted his fate long ago and knew that he could have a harem filled with many gorgeous wives and concubines so the decision didn't really bother him at all.

'Our agreement will only commence once the princess is wed to my son.' said Omri with a finality that left no room for negotiation.

Eth-Baal looked shocked and cried out in surprise: 'But, your majesty, my people are starving now!'

'Then get your daughter here quickly and you can leave with a bride-price four times the norm for a woman of her position, I am sure you can feed a few villages with that alone and then we can begin trading in earnest.' Omri's tone was cold and calculating, he wanted to hold on to the upper hand for as long as he could.

'She can be here within a week,' hissed the king of Sidon, 'I hope she pleases you my king.' Bowing down low again and touching his forehead to the marble floor, he appeared to be defeated but he knew that Omri drove a hard bargain and was prepared from the onset to marry his beautiful yet extremely defiant daughter to the Israelite prince, he sold her as he would have sold a batch of his nation's purple dye and he felt no remorse for doing so.

After Eth-Baal had left, Ahab turned to his father and casually asked: 'Do you think that guy is both the High Priest and the king of Sidon?'

Omri sat contemplatively for a while before answering that he was doubtful that they could trust the man but that he had heard rumours that Eth-Baal was both king and priest, 'An unusual situation as the people don't normally mix religion and politics together, but Phoenicia is said to be the land of mystic and magic.'

They sat together for a while longer enjoying the comfortable silence, each one thinking about the morning's events and then Omri spoke: 'I hope you understand that it is for the good of the nation that I agreed to the marriage and being a prince, it is your duty to put Israel first and your personal desires second.' He looked over at his son and smiled apologetically, 'It comes with the territory.'

'I hope she doesn't look like an old camel or worse.' laughed Ahab, 'If she looks like her father, I might have to cut her nose off to make an improvement to her face.' His green eyes twinkled mischievously as his lips twitched upwards in an amused grin that put Omri's mind at ease.

'You can always keep your eyes closed or cover her face with a large cushion.' countered Omri jokingly and they both burst into laughter.

'This coming from the man who has a great beauty as his only wife.' chuckled Ahab as he patted his father on the back and stood to leave the throne room to find his trusted friend Judas and give him the news of his betrothal. He intended to drink a lot of wine with his friend and enjoy his last few days as a single man sampling all of the available female flesh he could.

CHAPTER FORTY-EIGHT

The anticipation raced through Samaria. The people were all excited, rejoicing and cheerful about the upcoming festivities, the banquets and marriage of their handsome young prince to the famously fair Phoenician princess.

Wedding preparations were underway everywhere, baskets of flowers were brought into the palace decorating the halls and the many rooms and scenting the air with their lovely sweet perfumes. Meat was being prepared and several more cooks and servants were taken into the palace kitchens to keep the constant demand for the fine foods and delicacy's flowing out of the kitchens timeously during the huge wedding feast.

Omri ordered the sacrifices of ten perfect bulls daily to show the Golden Calf god the nation's gratitude and appreciation for the peace and prosperity they were experiencing and he personally attended all the evening services at the high place that he had ordered to be constructed when they first arrived in Samaria.

The altar was made out of rough uncut stones in a perfect square on top of a hill. There were bull horns around the altar at each corner that corresponded perfectly with north, south, east and west so that the centre of the altar, where the bulls were to be slaughtered, was symbolically the centre of the world. It had steps leading up to the top so that the High Priest could go up to the top and be closer to the god or if the Golden Calf desired, the god could descend easily and walk amongst his subjects during their worship.

Oak trees had been planted encircling the base of the altar so that the high priests and worshippers could stand under the sacred trees and their prayers would be more pleasing to 'Apis', the Golden Calf.

Little Athaliah was only five years old but already a great beauty, she was doted on by everyone from the lowliest palace slave to her older brother Ahab and both of her parents. No one could refuse her anything, she was denied absolutely nothing her heart desired and Leah was often worried that she would become spoiled and selfish, but her angelic, blue eyed smile would dash all of Leah's worries away swiftly. Her deep blue eyes reminded Leah of sapphires sparkling richly and her thick wavy auburn hair contrasted gorgeously against her creamy soft complexion drawing many loving smiles. Her excitement and happy childish squeals echoed around the palace as she darted around after her pet cats along the many wide corridors and played hide-and-seek with the palace staff and other children.

'Omri, why have you never taken any other wives?' It was very late and Leah was lying in bed with her husband after their passionate lovemaking one evening. She knew it was common for kings to have a harem filled with many wives and concubines. She had heard of royal wives that had only ever seen their husband once in their entire marriage and the thought filled her with gratitude that she had not been locked away in a compound that would have felt to her like a prison.

'I didn't think I needed any more women around me,' he answered lightly, 'I can barely keep up with you.' he chuckled.

'But my love, we only have little Athaliah and I have not conceived in the five years since her birth! You need sons to keep your line strong and secure!' Leah had been worrying about her inability to conceive again and felt like a failure in their marriage for some time. In their culture it was seen as a curse for a woman to be barren and the more children a woman bore, especially sons, the more honour she was given. Leah was heartbroken that she had failed to provide Omri with many sons to safeguard his future dynasty.

'Think about it Leah,' chided Omri gently brushing a stray curl from Leah's forehead with his fingertips; 'Ahab is strong and soon to be married and will sit on the throne after me someday, and then his sons after him. Too many brothers often ends up in jealousy, corruption and deceit within the palaces.' He paused as she sat up to look at him seriously before he continued: 'I have heard many terrible stories of the heir to a throne killing all of his male siblings and relatives just so that he won't have any rivals plotting to usurp him! In light of that, maybe we have the best situation here, in the next generation when Ahab's son succeeds the throne, he won't be killing any of our sons or our grandchildren or even vice versa.'

Omri smiled tenderly as he tried to comfort his wife. He loved her deeply and wished she could understand the dangers that came along with the power he wielded. Someday he knew he would not be around to protect her, she was so much younger than he was, and he silently appealed to his Golden Calf god to keep Leah safe through the dangerous web of politics and deception.

CHAPTER FORTY-NINE

The morning of the much anticipated wedding dawned. It was a perfect day with clear blue skies and honey-coloured sun-shine. There was a buzz of busy activity everywhere Leah went, the preparations were all being finalized and the thrill of the excitement and anticipation crackled through the crisp clean air.

The smells coming from the palace kitchen were delicious as the aromas of lamb slow roasted in rich goat's milk, garlic and sweet herbs, figs and dates smothered in honey and many more mouth-watering delicacies from Phoenicia were hanging heavily on the gentle easterly breeze.

The high place was surrounded by all the citizens of Samaria leaving an opening for Jezebel to be carried through on her sedan chair, surrounded by her entourage. Omri and Leah were seated in the front row of the spectators surrounded by their guards and watched over carefully by Jared and Judas who held their spears crossed over one another behind the king and queen.

Omri leaned over and whispered in Leah's ear softly, 'I remember standing there like that. It was one of the most terrifying moments of my life.' He smiled at her playful response as she said: 'Why? Omri, the great and fearless general, victorious in many bloody battles and king of all Israel was afraid of a young slip of a girl?' They turned to the front and Omri adopted his stern, hard expression reserved for everyone except those who had a special place in his heart.

Leah smiled to herself as she sneaked a quick look at his firm countenance and thought lovingly, 'The people see the strong and strict Omri and they love you for it but they don't know you like I do, they don't see your love and tenderness beneath the hard exterior.'

Ahab stood in front of the altar beside the High Priest and felt truly nervous for the first time in his life. His hands were sweaty and he felt like he could not breathe, he was sure that Dan had tightened his armour on too tightly and it was constricting his chest. He had to keep reminding himself of the political advantages for marrying this unknown woman. The trade and peace treaty between Israel and Phoenicia was being sealed at that very moment. 'It's for Israel. It's for the good of the kingdom.' he repeated silently to himself as the entourage approached him with loud singing, dancing and rejoicing.

Jezebel sat motionless in her chair as it swayed awkwardly towards him. He could not make out the features of her face as her head was covered with a long dark veil. When the chair was lowered in front of Ahab, he held out his hand and Jezebel blindly took it, accepting his symbolic protection and provision. She stood beside him and they were married by the High Priest who removed Jezebel's veil to crown her the new princess of Israel.

'Welcome, princess of Phoenicia! I have heard rumours of your great beauty, and for once…the gossips were right.' said Ahab with relief flooding through his entire being as he looked at his wife's beautiful face for the first time.

Jezebel dropped her head faintly in the proper submission and smiled sweetly, her luscious red lips parting seductively showing her perfectly even white teeth. Her eyes were golden in colour, like a lioness', dangerous but hypnotically captivating and unusual, framed by black luscious long lashes, her long blond hair hung in golden curls down her back to her narrow waist like spun sunshine. She wore a red coloured robe made of the finest Sidonian silk that contrasted with her perfect creamy complexion and clung to the sensuous curves of her delicate body. She moved gracefully like a leopard, slow and seductively.

Ahab was instantly captivated by her flawless beauty from the moment he laid eyes on her, all thoughts of her ugly father were banished as he stared in admiration at the stunningly beautiful woman who was now his wife and he thanked whichever god was paying attention for his good fortune.

To Be Continued...

Author's Note

Forgotten Kings is a fictional account of the kings of Israel based on historic fact.

I have taken what we know about these kings from the archaeological findings, as well as what we are told in the Bible and given them personalities that I hope will make their forgotten stories intriguing and unforgettable.

It is important to remember that the book is fiction and the events, places and characters are based on historic fact. The dates and rule of kings are as accurate as possible and any mistakes are mine alone.

This book is about three men who either by birth, circumstances or murder became the king of Israel and covers the history of the kings from 884 B.C. onwards.

Rehoboam was King Solomon's son and refused to lower the taxes, oppressing the people of the United Kingdom of Israel because of his love of luxury.

Jeroboam, a former commander in King Solomon's army, had tried to reason with Rehoboam but in his arrogance, Rehoboam refused to listen and ten of the twelve tribes split away under the leadership of Jeroboam and formed their own kingdom in the North called Israel, leaving only two tribes in the South as the Kingdom of Judah (named after the largest of the two tribes).

Nadab was the second king of Israel succeeding his father King Jeroboam, who did in fact establish the kingdom of Israel and built the capital of Tirzah, or the Northern Kingdom as it is sometimes called.

Baasha the third king of Israel, did also in fact begin as a captain in King Nadab's army, he assassinated Nadab after he had been on the throne for only two years during a similar siege at Gibbethon.

Baasha claimed the throne for himself and killed all of Jeroboam's family to secure his claim to the throne. He ruled for twenty-four years and during that time he did in fact fortify the city of Ramah and was double-crossed by his ally Ben-Hadad of Assyria, who had joined forces with Judah's king, Asa after a bribe was paid by the latter to Ben-Hadad to repel Baasha from the city of Ramah.

Elah succeeded his father Baasha and ruled for only two years. All we know about him is that he appeared to be a drunken reprobate and was killed with Arza (his chamberlain) by Zimri at Arza's house during a night of drunken debauchery.

Zimri was in fact the commander of half the chariots. I have taken the liberty of filling in the blanks left by the historic records. There is no record of whether or not Zimri actually took part in the siege at Gibbethon and returned to Tirzah to assassinate the king or if he was in Tirzah all along. I thought it would work better in my story to leave him behind and bitter in Tirzah during the siege. He did murder the existing king, Elah, and claim the throne of Israel for himself.

All of Baasha's line was in fact killed by Zirmri within the seven days that he ruled in Tirzah before Omri arrived back from Gibbethon and besieged the city.

We are not told how General Omri heard about the death of Elah, but that he did hear and had returned to Tirzah from the siege at Gibbethon, which was 35 kilometres away, within seven days.

Omri did immediately surround the city and once Zimri saw that he was defeated, he set the palace alight around him, committing suicide and burning Tirzah, which was the royal capital of Israel (until Omri built Samaria) to the ground. Zimri was a man who made it to the very top and then lacked the character to remain there.

Omri was the General of the Army of Israel and was leading the siege at Gibbethon when Zimri killed Elah. He was proclaimed king by the army and for the first four years of his reign, Tibni, son of Ginath, contested for the throne and a civil war broke out. I have shortened the time and details of the civil war due to the fact that there was not much material to choose from to add to my account and I didn't want to bore the reader with a lengthy drawn out affair.

All we are told about Tibni is that half the people followed him and four years after Zimri burned Tirzah down, Tibni died. I assume that he died of natural causes as it doesn't say anywhere in the records that he was killed or poisoned or anything other than that 'he died'. The fact that the text merely states that 'he died', rather than that he was killed may imply that his death was natural – in effect, that he had become so insignificant that killing him was unnecessary.

The civil war died with him and Omri ruled for a total of twelve years. The first six years of his reign he ruled from Tirzah trying to rebuild the burnt city but when that proved to be an impossible task, he bought a hill from a man named Shemer for two talents of silver and built Samaria.

Omri named his new capital Samaria after the man who had sold the hill to him and the word Samaria also means 'wreath'. It was established as the new capital of Israel and is said to have been extremely beautiful and scenic. 'The city on a hill', as it was also known was so famously beautiful and prosperous, the likes to rival its counterpart Jerusalem.

Omri was a great military strategist who was famously successful, he was the first king of Israel to maintain a strong and stable government, yet the Bible pays him little attention. Political success in the eyes of the Bible writers, counted little if the individual had turned away from God.

Omri was so well known that in 732 B.C. Tiglath-Pilser III and also Sargon II in 721 B.C. (both Assyrian kings) attached such importance to the reign of Omri that they referred to Israel as "Omri-Land" about one hundred and fifty years after his death.

Omri's son Ahab inherited a prosperous kingdom from his father and ruled for twenty-two years.

He was married to Jezebel from Phoenicia, the daughter of Eth-Baal, the high priest and king of Sidon. The marriage was arranged by Omri during his reign to secure a politically advantageous peace and trade treaty with Phoenicia.